Robert George III

ISBN-13:978-1543136739
ISBN-10:1543136737

Cover Design: Crystell Publications
Book Productions: Crystell Publications
We Help You Self-Publish Your Book
(405) 414-3991

T...R...E...A...S...O...N

THE ULTIMATE BETRAYAL

A street fictional novel written by Robert George III that's guaranteed to go down in history as one of the best Urban Tales ever told. A certified banger! Finally, a story that will allow you to live your imagination... if only for a moment.

By: Robert George III

Robert George III

DEDICATION

I dedicate this book to every real nigga, gangsta, ride or die bitch, drug dealer, and stick-up kid across the muthafuckin world...this book is for you niggas. Especially you muthafuckin haters, if y'all only knew the motivation I get from knowing you fuck niggas is awaiting my downfall. Keep waiting because I'm not going anywhere, I'm here to stay as long as these checks keep piling up. And I would like to send an extra dedication to each and everybody who helped raise, shape, and mold me into the man that I am today. Whether you were family, a baser, drunk, prostitute, street nigga, or just a community leader of some sort...thanks for everything, I love you all. If it wasn't from those memories, then I wouldn't be able to share these gangsta ass stories with the world that I know y'all love so much. It will always be my pleasure to represent all of you muthafuckas who's afraid and still don't have a voice. So, in closing! I leave you with these few words; TRUST NO ONE!!!

Sincerely,

Robert George III

"The Mayor".

ACKNOWLEDGMENTS

First and foremost I would like to give praise to the Almighty where all praise is due. Thanks for the talented gift you blessed me with to be able to tell stories of such magnitude. Such a gift can only be given by the creator.

I also want to thank my team, TRAPHOUSE PUBLICATIONS 863. Y'all did your thang, and I love the way y'all handled yourselves marketing and promoting my books. Especially my assistant, who is the C.E.O. of the company and my best friend, Victoria Martin. Without you baby girl none of this would even be where it's at today. Thanks for keeping a real nigga focused and I love you.

I also want to thank all of my ex's, this list is way too long to start naming, but you muthafuckas know who you are. It was all of y'all thirst and greed that encouraged me to create these treacherous characters, especially the ones played in my book. Stop wanting every nigga you see that looks good, who got money, and is knee deep in the streets. Yes, I'm talking to you muthafuckas who ain't go ride for a real nigga when he needs you.

To my nephews and all of your soldiers, especially that young nigga Duke! "Bang, Bang, Muthafucka Bang. Oh yea, G-Man, how could I forget about you? You my big bro and I love you nigga. I remember when the whole city wanted to be like you, including myself. And Sporty Boy, I don't blame you for not being the role model and big brother I wish you could have been. I still love you nigga.

"T Muthafuckin G" tighten up sis. It's left up to us to hold the family down and keep them crazy ass kids in line.

And I know I missed a lot of people, but most of y'all are characters, so you have to read the story to see if I looked out.

For all of you muthafuckas who know me and know what I'm about, then y'all know how I feel about being locked down for toting that heater; I RATHER GET CAUGHT WITH IT THAN WITHOUT IT ANY DAY!!!

Sincerely,

R.G.

CHAPTER 1

A muthafucka once said; If it was meant to be, then nothing or no one could stop it from being. Damion thought as he sat outside of Tenille's trap house on the east side of Bartow, trying to geek himself up to run up in that bitch and lay everybody ass down, flat on their shit.

Even though Damion fucked with Tenille on a so-so basis, everybody was a suspected victim when it came to him eating. And at the moment, Damion had the inside scoop on Tenille's financial strong hold. One of his workers admired Damion's gangsta so much that he was willing to set up the nigga who's been putting bread on his table so his family could eat.

It was one thing about the streets, they didn't respect the good. Niggas respected fear, and that's exactly what Damion had in everybody's heart...fear. So, he used it to his advantage.

Malcolm's ticket to another life would soon come for his treachery. Damion knew that after he did what he had planned for Tenille, he couldn't afford to have any unloyal ass nigga rat him out and send him up the road to do a hundred years.

Contemplating on masking up or not, Damion threw the mask back inside the duffle bag he had strapped across his chest. Cocking back both .45 Berettas, Damion was as ready as ever. He knew that he had to go extra hard because it was a whole house of certified goons and go gettas. Especially Tenille, who was rumored to have bodied a few niggas in his younger days. But since he's been plugged in, fucking with the dope game, he hasn't indulged in that wild shit in a minute. So everybody looked at him to be pussy, especially them new niggas.

But Damion was from the old school. He was the true definition of a goon. He didn't care If you was a killer or whatever, he didn't give a fuck about none of that shit, it was dog eat dog with him. As Damion silently counted to three, he forcefully placed his size twelve Timberland boots, dead in the center of the front door, knocking it completely off the hinges, startling everybody inside. He caused them to panic for a split second, as they all thought it was the police. But, when they saw it was Damion, one of Tenille's workers quickly tried to reach for the sawed off twelve gauge that was sitting next to him on the couch. But, before he could get it in his grip, Damion sent two shots..."BOC! BOC!" hitting him dead between the eyes, killing him instantly. Busting another shot, Damion caught another one of Tenille's goons as he tried to take off down the hall, catching him with a single shot in the back of the head.

"Now if anybody else move, y'all fuck niggas go get the same thang!" barked Damion in a calm but evil demeanor, like this was something he did on a daily basis.

It was only two of them left to apprehend, as far as Damion knew. Then he spotted Malcolm's bitch ass, and snatched him up off the floor at gun point. Even though Malcolm had set up the lick by calling Damion, letting him know when Tenille was coming to re-up his trap. He was about to know first-hand how a real nigga handled a fuck nigga. Damion threw Malcolm the zip ties and told him to tie their asses up...both hands and feet. As soon as Malcolm was finished, he looked towards Damion for approval. But what he got was far from approval as Damion pointed the

.45 at Malcolm's chest and pumped five shots..."BOC! BOC! BOC! BOC! BOC!" into his heart, blasting Malcolm's body clean off his feet, landing his now dead body on top of Tenille leaving only Tenille and his right hand man K-Boy to deal with.

"God damn, Damion! What the fuck is all of this shit for?" screamed Tenille in a panicked tone of voice.

"Nigga, shut the fuck up. You know what it is. Now, you can make it hard on yourself, or you can make it easy." said Damion as he snatched Tenille from up under Malcolm's dead body, sitting him in a chair.

"Where the work at nigga?" asked Damion.

"It's on the table. Just get that shit and leave." replied Tenille.

"Nigga, you think I'm dumb? I know it's more dope in here than that! Now, I'm going to ask your ass one more time before I put a bullet in your man's K-Boy's head."

"Man, I promise you, that's all of it right there!" exclaimed Tenille.

"Alright then, I see you think I'm something to play with!" said Damion as he walked over to K-Boy and aimed the .45 at his head.

"Come on Tenille, give that nigga the work!" pleaded K-Boy as he spoke his last words, catching one to the dome..."BOC!"

"NOOOOOOOOOO!!" screamed Tenille as he just witnessed his main man and best friend get killed.

Still not believing all this, Tenille was about to go in shock until Damion caught him upside his head, slapping the shit out of him with his pistol.

"Tenille, you know I'm not playing with you. Now, do you wanna live fuck nigga, or do you wanna die? I'm giving you ten seconds to tell me where that stash is at or I'm just going to take my lost and grab the little work on the table." said Damion.

Tenille knew exactly what that meant. Not wanting to die like everybody else, Tenille thought it over hard for the little time he had to spare, trying to figure out how he was going to bounce back from a ten brick loss.

"Six, five, four, three, two..." counted down Damion as he was interrupted by Tenille.

"Okay, okay! It's in the second room on the left. As soon as you enter the threshold, pull the rug up and the floor board comes up as well. It's all there, just get that shit and go!" begged Tenille, as he gave up everything he had to his name. Knowing he went all in on this shipment, it was every damn penny he had.

Damion pulled Tenille out of the chair and dragged him down the hall just in case he tried to haul ass and hop out of the trap.

"I hope this nigga don't think I'm going to let his ass live! Because if he did, he had to be the biggest fool alive. All he did was buy himself an extra minute or so to get his soul right with God." Damion thought to himself.

Dropping Tenille down in the hallway face first, Damion hurried up and went to work as he opened up the door and snatched the rug up. He pulled the floor board up and just like a magician, them bricks were as white as snow. Damion snatched them all up and put them in the duffel bag he had across his chest.

"God damn! I didn't know this nigga was eating like this!" thought Damion as he zipped the bag up and headed back out of the room into the hallway where Tenille was still stretched out across the floor.

"Tell Satan I'll be there in a minute!" said Damion as he pumped Tenille's body full of led, only stopping at the sounds of sirens blaring in the far distance.

"Dammit, let me get the fuck out of here!" thought Damion as he opened the duffle bag back up and grabbed the ski mask out that he had refused to wear. Putting the mask on, making his escape out of Tenille's trap house, he jumped into the stolen Dodge Durango he had parked two houses down. People looked on in disbelief as he sped off.

Scared to death, they knew the devastation of what just happened inside of their neighbor's house. Even though they knew he sold drugs, they feared for his life at the moment because he was a good neighbor and always looked out for those of them in need.

As they whispered upon themselves, old man Mr. Larry who lived directly next door, made up his mind as he took off heading inside. Not knowing what to expect, but hoping he was able to help if help was needed.

CHAPTER 2

As the police arrived after the disturbance call of gunshots they'd just received only five minutes ago, there were crowds of people outside just standing around, blocking the road. They eventually made a clear path for the police, pointing directly at the house where the shots had come from. Once the police made it up to the house, he noticed the door had been busted and immediately called for backup.

"We have a possible two-eleven in progress, need assistance at 1732 East M.L.K. Avenue." said Officer Fulwiley as he drew his service weapon and proceeded into the house. Noticing the first dead body, Officer Fulwiley walkie-talkied the call in notifying the incident, asking for immediate medical assistance.

Checking the pulse on the corpse, Officer Fulwiley moved on. He knew it was nothing he could do as he checked the next body, only getting the same results. Not taking anything for granted, he headed on down the hallway where he saw another body with a hole in the back of his head, lying in a pool of blood. Checking his pulse, he was dead as well.

"This is the police, if anybody is here please acknowledge yourself or else I will be forced to shoot on sight!" warned Officer Fulwiley, opening up the first door to the left. The room was clear, as well as empty so he didn't have to do much of a search. Checking the next room on the right, which was the bathroom, it was clear as well. As he made his way down the hall to the last door on the left, he noticed it was open.

"Is anybody in there?" asked Officer Fulwiley more to himself than anybody as he noticed what looked to be a kilo of cocaine. He kneeled down and picked it up. Taking his knife out, he plunged a hole in the wrapping and tasted the substance on the tip of his blade, and instantly, his face went numb.

Officer Fulwiley hurriedly undone his uniform shirt and stuffed the kilo down inside his pants, putting his shirt back inside his pants.

"Ain't no way in hell this was going to evidence!" he thought, starting to ponder in his mind who he could drop the dope off on, and that's when he heard muffled cries coming from inside the walk in closet.

"Come out with your hands up...before I start shooting!" screamed Officer Fulwiley demandingly, in his most convincing police voice. That's when two of the baddest bitches Officer Fulwiley had ever saw came crawling out of the closet. Both bitches were drenched in tears, with their eyes all puffy and swollen from crying.

Officer Fulwiley saw the fear in both of their faces as he tried to talk to them, but all they did was hold each other as they shaked and shivered in one another's arms.

"Ma'am, could you please tell me what happened here?" asked Officer Fulwiley.

"I don't know!" said Moneisha as she held her head up, looking the officer dead straight in his eyes, letting him know that she didn't really have a clue to what the fuck really happened.

"All I know sir, is that we were about to get ready to put on a performance for this guy that we met at the club where we work, and all of a sudden there were gun shots. So we hid in the closet, and when we were about to come out, thinking it was all over with, we heard someone coming. So we stayed hid and came in here. But we were so afraid, so we didn't move or say anything. Then after a few minutes, we heard more gun shots. They were so close, we thought they were shooting at us." said Chineir, who was looking at the officer, happy that he was there.

She felt relieved, but what she didn't know was that she had done mesmerized the officer as well. He looked at them both back and forth, not believing these two bad bitches standing in front of him was identical twins. The only difference they had was their hair styles. Moneisha wore hers short, like a boy with waves and all. Chineir wore hers long. I mean naturally long where it came down to her ass. But she kept the sides shaved with designs and shit. Both of them stood at five feet, eleven inches with the measurements 36-24-46, weighing 170 pounds, yellow skinned with a set of dimples that gave them that Cabbage Patch Doll look. They both were standing in front of Officer Fulwiley in nothing but their work clothes.

Each wore a see thru bikini top and matching panties that was made out of clear liquorice candy, with eight inch red bottom stilettos on. Officer Fulwiley was able to see their hard nipples as they stood out damn near an inch. He couldn't help himself as he grew a hard on. But, he held it together as he asked them both did they have any other clothes to put on. He watched them hurry to their carry-on bags and slid into a one piece dress that was all black.

"Damn!" was all Officer Fulwiley could say as he thought about how bad these bitches were.

"I need to ask you; do you have any relations to anybody here?" he asked.

"Like I told you already, we met them at the club where we work. We don't even know their names. They gave us five grand up front and was going to give us five more once we were done, as long as we continued to entertain them. So, no. There's no relation...just business!" said Chineir.

"Okay, I'm about to walk y'all outside to my car, so I need y'all to look forward because you don't need to see what's out there!"

"Okay!" said Chineir and Moneisha at the same time, wondering what it was they were about to witness.

CHAPTER 3

The sound of his cell phone awoke Devell immediately as he recognized the call tone by Plies; Chopper Zone. He knew it was his main man Damion.

"But why in the fuck was he calling at four thirty in the morning, something had to be serious!" thought Devell as he answered the call. Under any other circumstances, he would've ignored the call, especially with what he had going on at the moment. He had finally got the bitch Kosha Davis to stay the night, and he wasn't playing with the bitch either. Devell's been beating in her pussy since ten o'clock the night before.

"What's up fam?" answered Devell wanting to know what the emergency was.

"Bro, I need you to come and scoop me up...like ASAP!" spoke Damion.

"Awe fuck! Nigga, you sure you can't call nobody else? Because I'm kind of tied up in something as we speak!"

"Nah bro, and besides, you're the only one I trust. And nigga you already know I wouldn't hit you up if it wasn't serious." said Damion.

"Okay, enough said fam. Just tell me, do I need to suit up?" asked Devell.

"Nah nigga. I done took care of that part. All I need is some transpo' because this raggedy ass splack cut off and won't crank back up."

"Damn fam! That shit sounds like one of those GPS shut downs! Boy, where you at?" asked Devell knowing he had to hurry up and grab his nigga.

"I'm on the back side of 540, right before you get to Spirit Lake Road, coming from Bartow."

"I'm on my way, I'll hit you up as soon as I get in the area. Just walk off a bit in case the police come to that splack!"

"I got you bro, just hurry up!" pleaded Damion all paranoid, thinking about the nine bricks he had in the duffle bag. Still mad because he had to leave one. But he had too, just in case shit hit the fan, he can always say it was drug related, knowing that brick of cocaine was going to be logged into evidence, and maybe his ticket to freedom if it ever came to that.

Of all the bitches Damion had on his team, even his baby momma Toya who use to be his ride or die bitch. He didn't trust nobody the way he did Devell, who was his right hand man. Both of them cut from the same cloth, having genuine love for each other, as if they came out of the same womb. Devell didn't even know he was about to get blessed just for the ride.

Damion already knew what he had for his main man

was gon' set him straight.

"Come on bro!" was all Damion was able to say to himself as he waited in silence, off the road about one hundred yards away from where he ditched the stolen Dodge Durango.

****

Old Man Larry was all too familiar with the game. He once was one of the biggest heroin dealer and pimp of his era. But fucking with them party animals got Larry caught up as he started to party extra hard himself, using his own drug supply. Then as soon as the crack epidemic hit, Larry had become a full fledge smoker, and it didn't take long before he ran through the millions of dollars he had accumulated in the game. Thank God for the prison bid he had served, because in those long five years behind bars, it was just enough time for Larry to kick his habit. Since he's been out, he's become a pillar in his community as well as a business owner owning his own lawn service, clothing store, and gas station. Even though Larry wasn't interested in the illegal street life, he still fucked with the young niggas that was getting it. Giving them the game from each and every angle, hoping to save them from the many diseases the streets brung.

For some reason, he liked Tenille and his crew. They reminded him of himself back in the days, only difference was; now-a-days they did too much flaussin. That was a no-no to Larry and other old school niggas from back in the days like Butch Ham, Jimmy Fanell, Sterling, Billy Bob, and Deborah Keys. They waited until the money was made, then they hung out like the true bosses they were. But, as bad as snitching was, Old Man Larry didn't blame these young niggas for stuntin the way they did. All they had was six months to a year in the game anyways. Compared to back in the days, where they went damn near ten years before the police even heard about them.

As Old Man Larry made it inside Tenille's spot, he noticed off rip three dead bodies in the living room. He ran to the first one, noticing it was the lil young punk Malcolm whom he never took a liking too. Checking him out, Larry seen that he was dead. Right beside him was Tenilles' main man, his cousin K-Boy. Checking him out, Larry saw that he had a pulse and that's when Joann came running through the door with her hand over her mouth in disbelief of what she was seeing. Never in her life has she ever saw a dead body.

"Baby here!" said Larry to Joann, handing her his keys, telling her to grab his truck and back it up to the front door.

Watching her leave, Larry went and checked another body. Seeing that he was dead, he ran through the house looking for anyone else. That's when he noticed two more bodies. One was Tenille, he instantly dropped down beside him and checked to see if he was alive, and just his luck, Tenille was still holding on for dear life. Old Man Larry was able to see that Tenille was hit badly, all over. Not knowing if there was much time left, he scooped up Tenille not even checking the other body that was up under him.

He rushed out the front door meeting Joann as she was backing up his F-150 pick up to the front door. Putting

Tenille on the back, he dashed back in and grabbed K-Boy then ordered Joann to take off, which she did obediently coming off M.L.K. onto Main, running the stop sign.

"Baby where in the fuck is you going?" asked Larry.

"To the hospital!" replied Joann.

"Nah baby! We can't take them to no damn hospital in Bartow. Jump on sixty and head to Brandon. If we take them anywhere in the county, they're surely bound to be charged with them murders back there. Baby you know how nasty these crackers are in Polk County." Larry said as he held on for dear life as Joann whipped the truck around and headed towards highway sixty, heading towards Brandon.

Larry knew he had a trooper in Joann. She's been riding with him for over thirty years. Even when he was on top, living the high life with his wife, Joann was still there as she stood in his corner. After the downfall, the drug addiction, the prison bid and all, Joann was still there when everybody switched sides. And now that the smoke was clear, Larry chose Joann to live the rest of his life with knowing that if something happened to him, she was down for the ride.

CHAPTER 4

As Devell came creeping up the road, he noticed there wasn't anybody else out. His headlights were the only ones visible, that's when he started flicking the brights back and forth, which was the code for all jack boys who needed a ride. Damion recognized the signal off top, that's when he came out and raced into the middle of the road, flagging Devell down, waving his arms through the air making sure he didn't pass him by. Devell stopped his Lincoln town car, making the twenty-eight-inch DUB spinners look like a Chinese fan in the night light, with that kandy brandy wine glistening in the dark.

"Damn bro, why you pushed your whip?" asked Damion.

"Because my bitch got my slider, so I had no other choice." said Devell as he looked at Damion's ungrateful ass as he turned his focus back to the highway, making a U-turn heading back towards his spot.

"My nigga, who you done hit?" asked Devell.

"Bro, I squeezed that nigga Tenille spot. I hit him for nine of them thangs!" bragged Damion.

"Nine what?" asked Devell, wondering if he was talking

about bricks, ounces, or pounds.

"Come on bro, you know me! I hit that nigga for nine bricks!"

"Damn nigga! Why you ain't put me up on the lick with you?" asked Devell, kind of heated because he had just put Damion up on a lick with the Haitians in the Haitian hole and had split everything fifty fifty with him. But here this nigga go doing solo licks...ALRIGHT!" Devell thought to himself as he tried to figure out his next move.

"Bro, you know I got you. You my fam for real nigga! It's just that this wasn't my lick so I had to get it like that, but here!" said Damion as he threw Devell two bricks.

"Damn nigga, wait till we get to the spot!" said Devell.

"Nah bro, swing me by my lil young bitch house and I'm good!"

"Which one?" laughed Devell, referring to the many young bitches Damion had. That nigga loved them little young, under age bitches.

"Alright bro, I got you!" confessed Devell already knowing he had a special thang for his lil bitch in the projects as he headed out towards St. Paul Drive.

"Tell me bro, what that nigga Tenille looked like when you stuck that fire in that nigga face?" asked Devell wanting to hear what happened because it was rumored that Tenille was known for bucking jacks.

"He ain't show no fear. As a matter of fact, the nigga wasn't about to give me shit talking 'bout the lil work on the table was all they had and that shit wasn't even a big eight!"

"Oh yea!" said Devell. "So what made the nigga give up the stash?"

"I put one in the back of that nigga K-Boy's head and gave that fuck boy ten seconds to live before I did the same to him." said Damion all cocky.

"You mean you bodied K-Boy?" asked Devell.

"Nigga I bodied everybody! K-Boy fuck ass, them two jits who always at his trap and Tenille. I didn't spare nobody!"

"So, who set the lick up bro?" asked Devell, worried. Because if he killed all those muthafuckas, it was just a matter of time before the streets or the police got wind of who did it.

"You know what's next, right? We gotta body your people on this one!" declared Devell, knowing his nigga done made the biggest mistake of his life.

"You late bro. I offed that fuck nigga on the spot. You know I don't leave no strings attached." confessed Damion.

"Which one it was?" asked Devell, being curious wanting to know which one of Tenille's workers went sour on him.

"That lame ass nigga Malcolm, and he ain't even see it coming!"

"Damn, you're a cold ass nigga bro." said Devell as he whipped his Lincoln into St Paul, sliding straight to the back. Damion dialed his lil tender's number, hoping she picked up.

"Hello, who is this?" asked Asia answering her phone.

"Baby it's me. Come and open up the door, I'm outside!"

"Okay, but come on before my momma wake up. I ain't trying to hear her muthafuckin mouth." said Asia as she hung up the phone.

"Alright fam, be easy nigga!" said Devell as he gave his nigga Damion some love by dapping him up before he got out of the car.

"I'm go get at you in a couple of days, you know where I'm at so if you need me just holla!" said Damion.

"That's what's up! Be safe nigga." said Devell as he slid back out of St Paul, making the twenty-eight inch spinners look like they were ice skating, knowing them lil nosey ass bitches was looking because them hoes never went to sleep in St Paul, one of the most dangerous project's in the whole Polk County.

****

Officer Fulwiley hurried up and stuffed the kilo of cocaine up under his car seat as he grabbed his incident report book to take notes as well as the digital camera out of the glove compartment. That's when police cruisers came rushing up from everywhere, blasting their sirens, jumping out setting up a crime scene perimeter. Ambulances pulled in, as well as fire trucks as they responded to the emergency call.

"I've been here over ten minutes and these cock suckers are just now getting here." thought Officer Fulwiley, thinking madly to himself at how the system treated the ghettos and the majority of all urban neighborhoods as if black lives didn't matter.

Making his way back out of the car, Officer Fulwiley noticed the all-black, unmarked Crown Victoria pull up. Already knowing who it was, Officer Fulwiley headed towards the car. When Homicide Detective Gerry Grant made it out, he saw Officer Fulwiley awaiting, ready to brief him on the accounts at hand.

"Who made first contact?" asked Detective Grant.

"I did sir." responded Fulwiley.

"Okay, walk me all the way through it, from the moment you arrived up until now!" ordered Detective Grant.

"Sir, when I pulled up, I noticed the door was off the hinges. I called back up immediately then proceeded inside. I identified myself, but no one answered. That's when I noticed the dead bodies. I checked them all for a pulse, but unfortunately they were all dead. I placed the necessary call in to life flight, just in case a life could be saved." said Officer Fulwiley. "Then I checked the rooms, they were all clear except the last room on the left...right here!" he said pointing. "As I made my way in I heard muffled cries coming from the closet. That's when I identified myself again, giving whoever was in there a warning that I would shoot if they didn't come out with their hands up. That's when two women exited the closet, all scared and trembling."

"You say, two what?" asked Detective Grant.

"I said two women! They're both in my car right now."

"So, we have witnesses?" asked Detective Grant.

"Yes sir!"

"Okay, get them to headquarters for questioning, and make sure you put them in separate rooms until I get there."

"I'll get on it right now, sir." said Officer Fulwiley as he took back off out of the house heading to his car, anxious to get back to the two bad bitches he had in his possession.

Detective Grant took a mental note as to how jittery Officer Fulwiley was acting.

"I got to see what's up with him!" thought Detective Grant as he turned his focus back to the crime scene, doing what he was best at, solving murders. Checking the position of the impact, Detective Grant was able to tell exactly where the shooter was at. Kneeling down, he also noticed a dried up path of blood that led all the way back out the door. "How-be-damn!" said Detective Grant as he realized there was another person here that was removed.

Checking the other bodies, he noticed another path of dried up blood. But it didn't last long as if somebody picked him up and carried him away. Now Detective Grant knew there were five bodies here instead of the three that was left behind. "But how did they disappear? Or why?" thought the detective as he realized somebody had to have move them.

"Everybody listen up. I want everybody outside questioned. If anybody looks the least bit suspicious, or even stutters, take their ass in to be interrogated. Somebody saw something, and I want to know who removed the two bodies from this crime scene." barked Detective Grant as he stepped aside and pulled out his phone placing the necessary call to his main man, the most reliable and trusted source of information he ever had, his own confidential informant.

"Hello!" said the other man on the phone.

"I need to meet you as soon as possible." said Detective Grant.

"When and where?" asked the informant.

"At the usual spot in forty minutes!"

"Alright, I'll be there." And just like that, their conversation was over.

CHAPTER 5

Damion couldn't even sleep, not to mention focus as flashes from the killings he just committed flooded his mind. Never have he ever killed someone. He had shot plenty of muthafuckas in his time, but taking a life! Damion never went that far. But after Malcolm had told him about the lick with Tenille, and how sweet it was, that's what he's been waiting so long to hear. It's been years that Damion tried to get the drop on Tenille, allowing his anger to build up had him anxious to pay Tenille back for betraying him ten years ago, setting him up to sell to an undercover agent. That landed him in the Feds, cutting Tenille's original commitment of twenty-seven years mandatory for the King Pin Act, to only six years in a medium custody facility. Damion knowing how the game goes, knew that this day would eventually come about. He was prepared, it was worth the gamble to him as he thought about all the money this nigga brung in on a daily basis. And all Damion wanted was an apology, like "Damn bro, I had no other choice! Them crackers was trying to hide me." But nah, Tenille even denied it all, not knowing that when Damion filed for his Freedom Of Information Act, his name, his C.I. number, and all was highlighted throughout his paperwork. And this nigga got the nerve to ride around in new Corvettes, Bentleys and Range Rovers like shit was all too sweet and dandy.

"I hope he enjoyed it!" thought Damion as he snapped back to reality. He tried to be calm and let his lil young tender get some rest being she had to go to school in the morning. But looking at her sexy ass body, all silhouetted under the silk sheets, Damion couldn't help himself any longer as he eased under the sheets with her and made his way down to her waist side, sliding his tongue across her thighs, tickling her in her sleep, making her body jerk to the sensitivity of his tongues touch.

Damion continued as he parted her legs and slid his head between them, sucking on her pussy lips making them stretch until he heard her moan. Looking up from under the sheets to see if she was awake, he noticed Asia was licking her own lips. That did it for him because she had them pokey looking fish lips that always looked like she was blowing you a kiss. Damion slid his index finger inside of her pussy while he sucked on her clit, rolling his tongue around it like a piece of candy. Before he knew it, he had three fingers inside of her, finger fucking the shit out of her. Asia had done came to life as she grabbed Damion by both ears pressing his head down, letting him know that she was about to climax. That's when Damion took his fingers out and began to tongue fucking her little tight, young, and inexperienced pussy, pulling her butt cheeks apart.

"Oooohhhh baby, I'm about to cum, I'm about to cum baby!" moaned Asia as she tensed up, holding Damion's ears while she built up one of the biggest nuts ever.

"Oooohhhh shit, here it comes, here it comes!" said Asia as Damion came up wanting to see his lil young tender cum all over herself. Asia began to rub her clit back and forth real fast as she screamed uncontrollably.

"Aaahhh fuck baby, here it comes!" which Damion nor Asia never saw this one coming as cum squirted out of her clit like a water faucet. That shit turned Damion the fuck on as he watched in amazement at his young tender do shit he only heard about. Standing on all fours, hovering over her body, Damion crawled his way up the bed until he was completely mounted over her. Asia was ready for him too, she loved sex just as much as a fat kid loved cake. She automatically lifted her legs up as Damion stuffed his thick, massive dick inside of her hot, soak and wet pussy. Not even playing with her, or wasting time, Damion plunged all eight inches inside, hurting Asia just a bit. But she loved it like that as she let out a soft moan, but really wanted to scream. But she knew she couldn't because it would wake up her momma, then all hell would break loose.

"Fuck me Daddy!" moaned Asia, sending Damion into a mad man trance, listening to his lil bad bitch talk dirty to him. He began to pump harder as he had her legs damn near in a pretzel position.

"You want this dick! You want this dick! Then throw that pussy back baby! Show Daddy who pussy this is!" said Damion as he pumped away, feeling himself about to cum.

Damion tried to slow down a lil bit to make the moment last, but Asia tight pussy wasn't going to let him. She used her pussy muscles and gripped Damion's dick inside of her, making him lock up as he tried to pull out, but he was unable to as he exploded inside of her, hoping he ain't just fucked up. But Damion was all in, he had just killed five niggas, what the fuck was he scared of as he dropped down beside her and dozed off.

Asia couldn't sleep. She was so happy. She had finally made this nigga nut inside of her. She had wanted a baby so bad, all of her friends had kids, or was about to have kids and here she was being treated like a lil girl. Always pulling out, talking about she was too young and shit. "But I got his ass tonight!" she was thinking about how her home girl Destinee taught her how to use her pussy muscles.

"So what, I let the dyke bitch eat my pussy! At least she taught me how to keep that dick inside." smiled Asia as she just laid there in Damion's arms, listening to his heavy breathing as she started to think of names for her baby that didn't even exist yet.

CHAPTER 6

As they pulled up to the Brandon Medical Center, Joann pushed the pick-up truck all the way up to the emergency entrance. Old Man Larry jumped off the back, raced inside yelling to the nurses that he had two wounded people on the back of his truck that needed medical attention immediately. Seeing all the blood on him, the nurse knew it had to be serious as she gripped a gurney and raced outside, followed by her co-worker who brung another gurney as Old Man Larry helped the nurses load Tenille and K-Boy's body onto them.

As they strapped them in and raced their wounded bodies inside the hospital straight to the E.R. for emergency surgery, they hooked their bodies up to the life support system, hoping to keep them alive until the doctors were able to perform whatever miracle they could on them. Joann and Larry stood outside of the emergency room, not able to sit down because Larry was too concerned about his two comrades while Joann was just concerned about Larry, never seeing him like this. She was hoping he was okay, but to be honest, it was turning Joann on like a muthafucka, as she felt her old pussy thump inside her panties from all the excitement.

"So baby, what do you think is going to happen?" asked Joann.

"I don't know baby, but I'm praying them young soldiers in there pull through. Because no matter what a man does, it's not enough to take his life away." said Larry.

"Yea baby, I agree with you, but who do you think it was? And why do you think they shot them all up?"

"Your guess is as good as mines baby. Hopefully these youngn's know and could get to the bottom of all this, you feel me baby? Because my ole' man always taught me that a fair fight was worth losing your life over, it was honorable. But these young cats these days just shoot each other up for no reason." said Larry.

"I never understood that baby!" replied Joann.

"Yea, me either. It's these sorry ass niggas who want what the next man has but is afraid to hustle for it, so they steal, rob, and kill for it. I never liked their kind. It's enough money for everybody out there, all they gotta do is get it like the next man!" said Larry as he began to get upset as he thought about how hard he hustled back in the days, and to let a nigga come and take it away, he wanted to war for the lil homies right now. But he knew it wasn't his battle so he calmed down a bit, awaiting on somebody to come out and update him on Tenille and K-Boy's condition.

"Damn! I hope I didn't help take them boys life by bringing them way to Brandon when I could have taken them right there to Bartow Hospital." thought Old Man Larry as he began to worry, and upset himself all over again.

****

It was turning day break outside when Devell slid by his baby mommas house. He noticed her car was there, but it was another car backed in behind hers. As Devell drove by, he noticed it was this lil nigga Skeeda's whip. A fuchsia pink Regal on twenty-six inch Davins.

"Oh yea! I know this bitch ain't trying me like this." thought Devell as he contemplated just passing on by and letting the bitch have her fun. But he thought otherwise and jumped right into his fuck it mode. *"This bitch wasn't about to be trying me, I pay her fucking bills!"* he thought.

Putting the Lincoln in reverse, he backed the car up in the yard and grabbed his glock nine and went straight ahead and kicked the living room door off the hinges. Devell didn't give a fuck, Tarrell knew all niggas were off limits, and by this nigga car being there he felt she was trying him.

Racing through the house with swiftness, Devell headed straight to the master bedroom, hoping to catch his baby momma in the ultimate act of betrayal. But what he got was far from what he was looking for as Tarrell and her home girl Pumpkin held each other tight, crying and afraid from the loud thud they heard from the door being kicked in.

"Who the fuck in here?" screamed Devell as he looked in the walk-in closet walking through it to the master bathroom. Seeing that no one was there, he came out and checked the other rooms.

"There's nobody else here!" screamed Tarrell, but Devell knew better because here his baby momma was, butt ass naked in the bed with another bad ass naked bitch. So what they were friends, and he knew it. *"What the fuck were they in the bed naked for while a nigga car was backed in his driveway?"* he thought, needing answers right away before both these hoes ended up dead.

Seeing that the whole house was clear, Devell marched back into the bedroom and went to going off.

"Bitch, what the fuck that nigga car doing at my house? And why in the hell y'all two hoes butt ass naked in my bed?" asked Devell, demanding an answer.

"Baby, I'm sorry. I wanted to tell you before but I was too afraid." pleaded Tarrell.

"Afraid of what?" barked Devell.

"Baby that's Pumpkin's man car out there. She drove it over here. The only two people that's been in here all night has been me and Pumpkin." confessed Tarrell.

"So, you telling me that you and Pumpkin is...I mean! Is...!" said Devell confused, as he got caught up in his words trying to get it out.

"Yes baby, I'm a lesbian. I've been gay way before me and you ever..." Before she could finish her statement, Devell bust a shot in the air..."POW!"

"Bitch, shut the fuck up! How you go try me like this? I told you I don't fuck with dykes or fags, and here you got another niggas bitch in my bed. Bitch, I should shoot both you muthafuckas." screamed Devell as he stormed back out of the house, not believing what he just witnessed. And come to think of it, he was about to ask Tarrell to marry him.

Walking by the nigga Skeeda's car, Devell stopped at the

custom Regal. He knew he had to have invested a lot of money in it because it was fiberglass throughout the inside, with speakers everywhere.

"Fuck this nigga shit!" thought Devell to himself as he unloaded his clip into the Regal, blasting Skeeda's Regal to pieces.

"Now let's see who's fucking who!" he said to himself as he jumped into his Lincoln, mashing the gas, making the super charged engine turn the twenty-eight inch spinners like a race car, tearing up the front lawn, sending grass and dirt all throughout Skeeda's shot out windows.

CHAPTER 7

By the time Officer Fulwiley made it to headquarters, he had done somehow developed a bond with the twins Moneisha and Chineir, wishing he could fuck both of them. But knowing the majority of the hoes out there wasn't trying to be fucked up with a cop, unless a nigga was a crooked ass cop and was out framing bitches just to fuck them. That's exactly when it hit Officer Fulwiley as he thought about trying to manipulate these two bad bitches to get inside their panties.

"Excuse me sir!" asked Moneisha. "Are we going to be alright? I already told you that we didn't see anything, so why are you taking us down?"

That's when Officer Fulwiley felt it was time to put his game into action.

"Well, ma'am. If y'all didn't do anything, then you would be cleared. But you must understand that this is a triple homicide investigation. There were three dead bodies in there, and somebody had to see something, which I'm hoping, because it would make things a whole lot easier for the two of you. But as of now, yes! Y'all are suspects!" said Officer Fulwiley.

"So, are we going to jail?" asked Chineir, scared to death knowing them man looking bitches was going to rape their pretty asses.

"Let's hope the best! As long as y'all be straight up with me, then I got y'all, but I can't help you if you don't let me know what's up." said Officer Fulwiley, hoping to scare them up, but not knowing he had done knocked the wall all the way down, especially after he kept on telling them about taking lie detector tests, hair samples, and finger prints.

The twins knew that they'd find out about them setting up the niggas who got killed. Supposedly it was five of them they had thought! But the officer said it was only three bodies, so two of them must have gotten away.

"I wonder if Odell is alright?" thought Chineir, wondering if he got away or if the other two niggas that brought them back from the strip club caught up with him. She continued in thought as she pulled her twin closer to her.

"Bitch, I'm go tell on his ass! Ain't no way in hell I'm going down because he's doing bad and want us to set up licks for his ass." said Chineir.

"Nah sis, We can't do that! Odell is our cousin and bitch that's just not right. And besides, you already know if we do that they'd black ball us out of all the clubs. Then how are we going to eat and get money to take care of momma?" said Moneisha.

"Bitch, if we get charged with them murders, we ain't go be working nowhere but in a fucking prison!" said Chineir, knowing that the sound of jail would scare the shit out of her sister. "And bitch, momma ass in a home. What she need us for?"

"Stop being so stupid Chi-Chi, you know we pay for her health care because you ain't have time to help take care of your own momma."

"I don't care about shit you saying, I'm telling on his ass. He shouldn't of have tried us like this. Anyway, I'm sick of being a nigga's flunky." said Chineir.

"Chi-Chi that's wrong. We can't tell on him no matter

what. All we have to do is be quiet and stick to our story, we don't even know shit! They just going to try and scare us like they do them people on First 48. Just remember that if they start making you feel uncomfortable, just say you want a lawyer." said Moneisha.

"Okay bitch." replied Chineir. "But I'm telling your ass, if these crackers try to charge us for anything, I'm telling on his ass, point...blank...period!"

"Just trust me, sis." begged Moneisha, as she held her twin in her arms to comfort her as they rode the rest of the way in silence.

****

Officer Fulwiley knew they were talking about something. He was hoping it was something that he could use to incriminate them. He had plans for their fine asses. "I could care less if they ever found out who killed them niggas. This badge help me protect my people and keep food on my table." thought Officer Fulwiley. "It had to be worth killing them over, because whoever it was, they left a whole kilo of cocaine behind. They must was thinking that if the police got the drugs along with the dead bodies, the case would be an open and shut one. They had to be looking at too much T.V. that shit didn't work like that. But, I'm glad they think so because now I got some major weight to get off..." smiled Officer Fulwiley as he wondered what them twins had so secretive to talk about knowing the ultra-sensitive recording devices the new police cars had would pick up even a pin drop.

CHAPTER 8

Devell was so upset with himself that he begin to notice he was driving around his mother's neighborhood in circles until he finally decided to pull into her driveway. Knowing it was Sunday morning, the whole house would be getting ready for Church. It was something they all did being that his family on his mother's side was full of Christians. He was the only outcast, and always been since he was eight years old.

But none of that kept Ms. Barbara Jean from praying for her baby boy, hoping God will one day deliver him from all the evils of the world. Walking through the front door, which was always unlocked because his mother believed whole heartedly that God would always protect her and her family.

"Hey Uncle!" said Lil A.C., his brother's son who was seven, with dreads that hung to the floor. They had to keep them tied up at the bottom. His daddy was Rastafarian, so he's been growing his hair since birth and studying the same faith as his daddy except on Sunday's his grandma took Church serious, and she wasn't trying to hear no child of hers or grandbaby was anything but Christian.

"What's up nephew?" asked Devell as he picked his nephew up and gave him a big hug. That's when he got rushed by all of the other kids that was there, like he was a bouncing gym. Losing his balance, he fell over onto the couch. He squeezed everybody real tight as he laughed along with the kids, realizing how much he had loved and missed them.

"Hey there boy!" said Ms. Barbara Jean. "Are you going to Church with us this morning?"

"Momma, I have something I need to talk to you about..."

"What you need, some money or something?"

"Nah momma, you know I don't need no money. I just want to talk to you about what's going on in my life." said Devell.

"I told you, I've been keeping you in my prayers. You know God says if the burden is heavy, he'd tote the load for you. All you have to do is come to him and ask for forgiveness, and confess with your mouth..."

"Yea momma, I know; confess with your mouth that you're a sinner and ask God to forgive you. You've told me that a thousand times, I already know!" said Devell.

"Boy, what's on your mind? You know you kids barely come by here and talk to me anymore!"

"I don't know momma, it's my baby momma. I just found out she's gay! I actually caught her with another woman in our house, in my own bed. I could've just killed her. I swear to God, that chick tried me for the last time!" exclaimed Devell.

"Listen at you, you sound like you ain't got no sense yourself. That's your child's mother and you talking about you want to kill her!" said Ms. Barbara Jean.

"I just don't know what I want to do momma, I really love that girl and I was about to ask her to marry me. But now I don't want to see her face again. How could I have been so stupid!" barked Devell angrily as he thought back to what he saw.

"Boy, if you love that girl wholeheartedly, then you have to forgive her. It shouldn't be nothing y'all can't get through...at least for the baby's sake!"

"I know momma, but..."

"Boy, don't but me. What you need to do is take your but on to Church."

"Momma, I don't got a Church that I go to, you know I've been caught up in these streets way too long! And besides, if I did have a Church to go to, I don't even have any Church clothes!"

"God says come as you are, and you're always welcomed in God's house. As a matter of fact, you can go with us, now go in there and put something in your mouth before we leave." said Ms. Barbara Jean as her soul was about to start leaping for joy as it tried to jump out of her skin. She knew her prayers had done finally made it home as she looked at her son. Staring at the back of his head as he went into the kitchen, a single tear escaped and made its way down her cheek.

****

As Damion got himself together, he had one of the basers from St. Paul take him to go grab his whip. He checked his phone messages only to witness he had done missed almost fifty calls. He began to check them and it seemed that everybody had already knew what had happened at Tenille's trap. But nobody knew or had heard from Tenille, like he just disappeared overnight.

At least nobody knew that Damion was the one who shook Tenille's spot down and left them all for dead.

As they made it to his crib, Damion was still caught up in deep thought as he thought of how he was about to jump all the coke he had in his possession.

"Here you go!" said Damion as he gave Cracker Joe a twenty for the ride, wishing he had some crack to give his ass instead of his cash, but Damion knew that he was about to have more cash than he ever dreamed of before the day was out.

"Grabbing the duffle bag that he had the seven bricks stashed in, both of his .45's, his ski mask, and all the accessories a nigga of his caliber needed to survive with. He went inside the two bedroom, one car garage row house that he used as a stash house. He usually put all of his guns there and the shit he accumulated from the licks he made. Plus, he kept his whip in the garage. He was the only person who had access to this spot. His own momma wasn't welcomed there. He couldn't trust the pressure niggas like himself would put on her. He knew what he was capable of doing if he snatched a nigga ole' girl up. "What a bitch didn't know they couldn't tell!"

Damion wasn't planning on staying that long. He had a lot of shit on his agenda, so a quick shower had to do as he picked out a pair of True Religion jeans, black Gucci V-neck tee shirt, and some all-black and red Gucci mid top sneakers along with his favorite YSL belt. Placing his phone on the charger, he hit the water. Letting the hot sprays massage his aching body, washing away the dried up sex from his young tender that was still on him. Jumping out of the shower and drying off, Damion didn't waste any time as he grabbed a pair of black boxer briefs and socks out of his dresser as he put on his clothes. He grabbed his phone off the charger, as well as his car keys and headed straight to his stash of guns that he kept in his custom built closet. he grabbed an AR-15 assault rifle, two extended one hundred and fifty round clips, and snatched the duffle bag up on his way out to the garage.

Hitting the alarm, disarming the hi-tech security system he had on his all black Dodge Challenger placing the AR-15 on the back seat, throwing the duffle bag right beside the assault rifle and jumped in cranking up the beast. The Hemi powered machine growled like a wild animal. Thumbing through his selection of music, Damion stopped on one of his favorite rappers; Yo Gotti, and went straight to track 7 pumping that "MY CITY" out as the six twelve inch kicker tried to bust out of the trunk. Damion hit the garage opener and backed out into the road, waiting to make sure the garage closed.

"Now, let me see who I can get to cop this work!" thought Damion as he contemplated on hitting his main man Doony-Hound up from Wauchula, knowing Doony was putting his thang down in Port Charlotte. But Damion thought otherwise, figuring Doony would want him to leave the work until he flipped it, and he just didn't have time to do none of that, he wanted his cash on deck.

As his neighbors looked on, Damion sped off, making the twenty-six inch all black Asanti's turn over, leaving a skid mark in the road. Then his phone begin to ring making the music idle down from the assist to talk hook up he had from one of the many features his car possessed. Checking the screen to see who the caller was, he noticed it was his cousin Skeeda. Skeeda usually fucked with the nigga Tenille them so he was wondering why the nigga was calling him. "It wasn't like they were on talking terms anyways." thought Damion as he answered the call, curious to what he had to say.

"What they do cuz?" answered Damion, letting Skeeda know off top that he knew who he was.

"Cuz, where you at?"

"What the fuck you mean where I'm at?" replied Damion.

"Cuz, a nigga just wet my shit up and I'm trying to get at him!" said Skeeda.

"Who cuz?"

"Some fuck nigga from Winter Haven. All I know is that nigga gotta see me cuz, straight up!" barked Skeeda.

"Cuz, you know where the nigga at?" asked Damion.

"Yea cuz, just come get me. I'll handle my own beef!' said Skeeda.

"You got some fire cuz?"

"Nah, bring me something and hurry up. I'm at the nigga

Ian spot in Inwood."

"So, when is you going to let me rob that fuck nigga?" Damion asked in a more serious tone.

"Come on cuz, you know them my peoples!"

"Nigga, I'm about to come through for you on some real G-shit and you talking 'bout them your peoples!" barked Damion in kind of an angry tone.

"Alright cuz, I got you. But nigga you go have to break me off when you hit his ass because that nigga strapped. That nigga fucking with about six or seven bricks every two days and he don't spend none of his money, so I know he's sitting on a fat ass stash. hell, I've been fucking with buddy for almost a year now, so you do the math!"

"Alright cuz. I'm on my way. But nigga be ready because I don't got no time to waste!" said Damion as he thought about dropping the .45's off on his cousin Skeeda.

"Shit, fuck that nigga! I rather it be him get jammed up with them shits than me." thought Damion as he headed towards the Inwood area to see what beef his lil cousin had going on.

CHAPTER 9

"Girl I told you not to even try that nigga like that!" spat Pumpkin. "You know that nigga ass is crazy! And look at what he did to my nigga's car. Skeeda is going to kill me when I get home!"

"I already know girl. I guess this the curse that comes along with what we do, you already know when Devell calms down I'm going to get the ass whipping of a life time." said Tarrell. "And trust me, I'm sorry about what my man did to your man's car. We should have been looking for that to happen! I'm glad it was just a car instead of one of us. I don't know what I was thinking about. Pumpkin, I should have known better. It's just that I'm tired of hiding who I am and I love that nigga so much girl, I want to share everything that I do with him!" pleaded Tarrell.

"Bitch, stop lying!" said Pumpkin. "Because you know damn well you ain't going to let that nigga fuck around!"

"You damn right I ain't, unless I'm there!" laughed Tarrell.

"So, you telling me that if Devell was with it, you was going to let him tap this?"

"You damn right, I was gon' sit there and watch him fuck the shit out of your ass!"

"Alright bitch! Don't play! You know how good this wet-wet is down here. I'll have that nigga sprung, you see how I got your ass!' said Pumpkin, bragging.

"Yea, with that fire ass head of yours!" laughed Tarrell.

"Bitch come here!" demanded Pumpkin as she pulled Tarrell into her embrace and stuck her tongue inside her mouth, giving her a long hard passionate kiss.

"Damn bitch, you trying to suck my tongue out of my mouth?" said Tarrell as she broke the kiss off, wondering what was up with her girlfriend and her roughness. But little did Tarrell know, she had done got Pumpkin all excited talking about how she wanted to watch her while her nigga fuck the shit out of her.

"Bitch, I've been waiting on this day!" she thought as she reminisced about how Tarrell was always bragging how her man's fuck game was. "Now it's my turn to sample the goods!" she thought, almost not hearing the horn blowing outside, knowing Skeeda was ready to go.

"Alright girl, make sure you call me later!" said Tarrell, not knowing what the fuck she was going to do. All she knew was that she was in love with two people and didn't want to live without either one of them.

"I will!" replied Pumpkin as she went outside and got in the car with Skeeda as he took off, following the tow truck out of there.

"So you said that nigga saw my car and bust down his bitch door looking for me?"

"Yea baby, I was so scared. I thought that he wanted to kill you! I don't know what I'd do without you baby, I'll go fucking crazy!" exclaimed Pumpkin as she was able to make a couple of fake tears slide down her face knowing Skeeda was extra sensitive. Just seeing the tears would break his ass down.

"Baby, it's okay! I promise you that I'm go see 'bout that fuck nigga. But what I need you to do is go on home and I'll catch up with you later." said Skeeda.

"Where are you going baby?" asked Pumpkin.

"I'm going to Ian's spot, I have a lil business to handle

so I'll have to get up with you later.

"So, what about your car, where are they taking it to?"

"They're taking it to Gabe shop to get fixed. It's all good baby, you know I got that custom insurance, so that shit gon' get fixed for free, you feel me!"

"Okay baby, because I know you was trying to get us that new house." said Pumpkin in her fakest concerned voice.

Skeeda's phone began to ring. As he checked it, he saw it was his cousin Damion so he hurried up and answered it.

"Yea cuz, what they do?" asked Skeeda.

"Nigga, where your ass at? I told you I didn't have any time to waste!" barked Damion.

"My bad cuz, I'm about to hit the block right now. You should see me about to pull up in a grey Lexus."

"Alright, I see you. Tighten up nigga because I'm too hot to be sitting still in one place." said Damion as he ended the call.

"Baby, I love you!" confessed Skeeda as he leaned over and gave pumpkin a kiss as he got out of the car and rushed over to Damion's whip. But, he didn't get in right away as he kept his focus on Pumpkin as she got out of the passenger side and walked to the driver's side, putting on one of her nastiest walks, slanging her ass from left to right like she was trying to break her hip.

Skeeda caught on quick, but he ain't say shit because he knew Pumpkin and Damion use to fuck around. He also knew that his cousin was mad at him for locking the bitch in, but Skeeda couldn't help it, *"Pumpkin was just a bad bitch that a nigga would do anything for to wife her."* he thought as he just let the moment blow before getting into the car.

"So cuz, you got that fire for me that I asked you to bring?" Skeeda asked.

"Yea, I got it nigga!" replied Damion as he reached into the duffle bag that was on the back seat and grabbed both .45's, handing them to Skeeda.

"These are for you cuz, you gotta always stay strapped. You never know when your life gonna depend on it!" Damion preached, happily to have tossed them heaters off on somebody else, knowing he had just bodied five niggas not even ten hours ago.

"So, where to cuz?" asked Damion.

"Just hit a few blocks and let me see if I can catch this nigga slippin!"

"So you saying, you gon' handle your business?"

"Hell yea!" replied Skeeda. "As soon as I see this nigga, I'm busting on sight, just watch."

"Alright gangsta, now you're talking my kind of talk!" said Damion as he sped off, bending corners. Hoping they found what they were looking for.

****

It was day light and the police, homicide, and special task force units was still outside of Tenille's spot as they begin to wrap things up. They weren't able to get any information to help them except; it was one person, he had on a mask and jumped in a big blue Dodge Ram truck that they had already located on Spirit Lake Road, abandoned.

"Where do I go from here?" thought Detective Grant as he prayed for a break in the case, hoping his informant would break the good news to him.

"Tape this whole area off and leave a patrol car on watch twenty-four-seven just to see who comes here. I don't give a damn who it is, arrest their ass on site and bring them to me. Somebody knows something, and somebody is going to tell me something! I'm heading back to the station." said Detective Grant as he hopped into his unmarked Crown Victoria and raced his way to the station, ready to interrogate the two bitches Officer Fulwiley had recovered from the scene.

"Them bitches better have something to tell me, or I'm going to fuck somebody up!" thought Detective Grant, wondering what strategy he was going to use to get what he wanted."

CHAPTER 10

"Excuse me sir, are you family to the two patients that were brought in here last night?" asked the doctor as he approached Old Man Larry and Joann with his nurse assistant on his heels.

"Yes I am!" replied Larry. "How are they doing?"

"Well sir, it was a close call. They both lost a lot of blood, and has not fully recovered from surgery yet. But we're expecting them to make a full recovery. Especially the bigger one, he took a shot to the head that went clean through, in and out, by passing any damage. Unlike the little one, he's a fighter! He took seven shots from a high caliber hand gun but still managed enough strength to cling on to survive. I'm hoping he have a full recovery as well without complications because one of the shell fragments wasn't able to be removed, it lodged into the same channel as the spine, and if removed it could paralyze him permanently. We found a blood match and replaced all of his bodily fluids back inside of him that was needed. Now, it's all up to him!" said the doctor as he looked at Old Man Larry and Joann for any sign of grief, but all they showed was sympathy.

"Is there any kind of way I could see them?" asked Larry.

"Yes you can, but please be mindful not to ask too many

questions. Try to let them rest as much as possible, we're not trying to send them into a shock, causing a coma!" said the doctor.

"I got'cha Doc, just let me see my nephews." said Larry.

"They're both in the same room. Follow me and I'll show you where." said the doctor as he led Larry and Joann around a series of curves and turns until they came to room 318.

"Just let Nurse Everett know when you're done." said the doctor as he led the nurse out, back down the hall to the reception desk for that floor, while Larry and Joann went inside the room. Joann stayed back towards the door where she sat down in a guest chair while Larry approached the first bed, seeing off top it was Tenille. He felt sorry for his lil soldier, but he was glad that he was going to make a full recovery.

"Damn youngin! The game damn near took your life away. Boy you must got a calling. Them bullets that went inside of you didn't kill you! God has got to have a plan for your life." spoke Larry softly trying not to disturb him like the doctor ordered as he begin to get all teary eyed, looking at all the tubes and bandages running throughout his body.

"Just get yourself some rest and heal. There's always time to retaliate and get revenge !" said Larry to Tenille, hoping to get some kind of indication that he heard him, but he got nothing but a steady beep from the life support machine, letting him know that Tenille was alive and that was good enough for him.

"Alright soldier, you get well!" said Larry as he went over to the bed where K-Boy was and unfortunately, he was in the same conditions. Tubes and bandages everywhere. But Larry gave the young soldier the same pep talk he had given Tenille, hoping to get a response, but still nothing.

Larry grabbed Joann by the hand and escorted her out of the room, down the hall to the receptionist desk where nurse Everett was and told her he needed to talk to the Doctor, it was very important. When the doctor showed up, Larry ran it down to him about how they needed to be logged in under John Doe's because people were trying to kill them. Because of life threatening circumstances they could do this under hospital policy. Larry knew what he had to do, he was about to go home, clean up, and head back over until these young cats was ready to leave.

"Doc, I'm their only family, so please, no visitors for them except their Uncle Larry Smith!" asked Old Man Larry as he got a head approval from the doctor.

"Doc, I have to head home, but I'll be back first thing in the morning with my proof of insurance and everything else you need to continue to care for them."

"That's exactly what I was about to ask you about!" said the doctor.

"Just give me until tomorrow and I'll have it all covered." said Larry already knowing what it was he had planned. All he was hoping for was that his young soldiers was awake when he got back because Larry was going to bust them right out of there.

****

Ms. Barbara Jean was so happy to see her son sitting beside her in Church. It was like the flood gates to Heaven had opened up. Everybody was shouting for joy and rejoicing in the name of God. Devell wasn't no stranger to the word, he grew up in the Church as a child, it's just the streets had got a hold of him at an early age and that's where he's been stuck ever since. He silently sang along with the gospel hymns the Church was singing. That's one thing Devell knew he'd never forget. Those songs were like chicken soup to a sick child's soul. Through the whole service, Devell couldn't get Tarrell off of his mind. How could she even try him like that? Had him wondering if she ever had a man over to the house. He kind of got upset, but quickly the mood was changed as the Church begin to sing; *I Just Want To Thank You Lord*. Which was his favorite Church song of all times. Devell just slumped back in his seat as he asked God to forgive him and show him a sign of what to do about his baby momma, because he did love her, and wanted her to be his wife. But now, he was wondering if he could ever trust her again.

After the Pastor led everybody in prayer, the Church was let out. It seemed as if everybody there had given him a hug. As they were walking down the steps onto the sidewalk, Devell noticed his main man's car cruising up the street.

"What that nigga riding around early for?" Devell thought as he sped up, hoping to stop him to see what was on the agenda.

Waving the all-black Dodge Challenger down, it gave the Church people sort of a menacing feeling as they watched the twenty-six inch Asanti's come to an abrupt stop right in front of the Church.

CHAPTER 11

Chineir was a nervous wreck as she sat in the ten by ten square foot room of an office. Separated from her sister, awaiting someone to come and interrogate her. Chineir knew the game all too well, even though she never been to jail or in a predicament like this before. She's watched enough T.V. to know exactly how it went down. As Detective Grant entered the room with her, it almost immediately seemed like her air was cut completely off. Walking to the corner of the room, he reached up and unplugged the camera, then pulled his chair up directly in front of hers, not even a foot away, looking Chineir dead in her eyes.

"I know you probably think that this is going to be one of those good cop bad cop routines where I'm going to get pissed and start flipping chairs and tables! Then someone is going to come in here and save you from me, like they're your friend!" said Detective Grant, "But I promise you, we're a million years from that happening. I want to make this as simple as it gets! We have three dead bodies, there's no witnesses or no suspects as of yet. But here we have you and your sister who was there at the crime scene, who claims they didn't see shit. At least that's what's been told to my officer who made it at the scene first. Now this can go either one or two ways. One, you tell me who the fuck it was who came up in there because I can tell by the look in your eyes that you set the shit up! I just hate you bitches who think you're all that. You're untrustworthy and as a result, lives have been taken." barked Detective Grant as he continued on. "Or two, you can be quiet, cry up a storm talking about you want a lawyer but at the end of the day, guess what? I'm going to charge you and that pretty sister of yours with three counts of first degree murder. Now. the choice is yours. So, what's it going to be?" asked Detective Grant.

"I want a lawyer!" said Chineir, knowing that it was best to keep her fat mouth shut, hoping her twin did the same thing, because these crackers knew how to twist your words up, so if you said nothing they knew nothing.

"So you think that this is a joke?" barked Detective Grant.

Chineir only ignored his tone of anger as she fucked around and smirked, taking Detective Grant's seriousness for granted. That's when he caught her with a straight jab dead in her big pokey lips, smashing them back into her face.

"Bitch, I don't see shit funny!" said Detective Grant, and that's when Chineir lost it. She went to swinging back at the detective all wild, catching him with a flurry of girly shots, none reaching their destination, but just the thought of this crazy bitch trying to assault him sent Detective Grant into attack mode. He reached his long lanky arms out and wrapped his massive hands around Chineir's neck, squeezing it as he lifted her clean off the ground. All she could do was kick her legs while she tried to pry his grip loose. But, she was no match, and she knew it as he continued to squeeze her life right out of her body. Chineir felt that this was it, so she hawked up a big ball of spit and spat it dead in the detective's face. Feeling better now that his shit was covered with blood and spit, she was ready to die now. But, her fate hasn't arrived just yet as the detective rammed her against the wall, making the back of her head smash the wall, knocking Chineir clean out. Once her body went limp, the detective thought he had killed her and rushed out of the room. But not until he kicked her in the kidney with his wing toes.

"This bitch got me fucked up! I hope she's dead because if not she's going to wish she was!" thought Detective Grant. "She might know how to fight physically, but I'm going to see if she know how to fight all these damn charges I'm about to put on her ass!"

Racing out of the room, Detective Grant left Chineir balled up on the floor, unconscious as he radioed Officer Fulwiley to clean up his mess, which he came to do immediately. But, when he saw the beautiful creature of a woman he only moments ago admired, battered up and laid out across the floor, it began to make his blood boil.

"What have this muthafucka done?" thought Officer Fulwiley as he tried to perform CPR on Chineir. He blowed air into her lungs and then pumped her chest forcefully three times, bringing her back to life on his first attempt. He grabbed her and sat her up in the chair.

"Listen to me, I'm going to get you and your sister out of here, okay! I'm sorry about all of this, I feel responsible. But trust me to get y'all away from here! I hope you didn't talk to him, he's as crooked as it gets. He's -- under investigation from the Attorney General's office for murder, corruption, and extortion. But, no one has come forth to testify against him. They're using me as a potential witness from when a detainee was murdered. Supposedly he was in interrogation with another detective but that's when they went to review the camera, and it was unplugged, just like the one is in here with you right now. You better consider yourself lucky!" said Officer Fulwiley as he helped Chineir out of the room to the holding cell where she would be protected until he went and got her sister.

"Should I tell her about the recorded conversation they had in my car, or wait until I have both of them together?" thought Officer Fulwiley, making his way back to the other interrogation room to get her sister.

****

"BOC...BOC...BOC...BOC...BOC..." was the sounds of gunshots heard from the .45 as Skeeda dumped round after round into Devell's body as he stumbled backwards onto the side walk. Seeing his life flash right before him, Devell wasn't about to go out like a pussy. He reached down and grabbed the .40 cal from his waist and pointed the massive hand gun at Damion's car, releasing two shots..."BOOM...BOOM!" before hitting the ground. One shot hit Skeeda in the shoulder ripping it apart, while the other one caught him dead in the face, blowing his brains out the back of his head onto Damion as he mashed the gas and cleared the area, not wanting any more bullets to enter his whip. He knew them bullets could hit anyone.

As Damion looked over to his cousin who was slumped in his seat, he knew it was over for him as brain matter hung out of the massive hole in Skeeda's head. After clearing about two blocks, Damion pulled over and pushed Skeeda's dead corpse out of his car onto the road, along with both .45's making sure none of that shit led back to him.

"Damn, I can't believe this fuck nigga just hammered my dawg!" thought Damion as he raced the Challenger out of town, knowing damn well he was going to have to lay low after this one. The police was sure to come after him with all them Church people as witnesses.

Placing a call in to his cousin, Trilla, who answered on the second ring.

"Hello!" her sweet voice answered, sounding like the singer Michelle'.

"Cuz, I'm on my way up there! And I'm loaded, so get ready!" said Damion.

"Alright cuz, I was just thinking about you too, me and Emma was laughing at your ass about that time you hooked that truck up to that nigga trailer and pulled it down the highway because he owed you twenty dollars. Boy, you be wilding out!" said Trilla.

"Cuz, you talking about that nigga Pimp! You know I don't play about that cash. I go too hard to get it, so I'm gonna go just as hard to keep it. You feel me? But it's all good cuz, I'm bout to make it happen so as soon as I hit Panama City I'm gon' hit you up." said Damion.

"Alright Cuz, you drive safe and I love you!"

"I love you too!" Damion replied as he ended the call, grabbing the blunt from the ash tray that he left there almost a week ago. It was just some reggie, but that shit was smoking like some fire ass Kush. Inhaling the smoke from a long ass drag, Damion's mind began to relax as he thought about the mill ticket he was about to make off them lames in Panama City.

****

The Ambulance made it on time as Devell had collapsed onto the pavement unresponsive. They hooked up the defibrillator to him on sight, blasting the electric volts straight to his heart.

"Again!" said the emergency responder, "Again...Again...Again!"

"Beep...Beep...Beep...Beep!" was the sound of the machine as it read a pulse.

"We have a pulse!" said the other emergency responder.

"This is a strong one here. Let's get him to the hospital. We may have to airlift this one to Tampa's Saint Joseph Hospital!" said the emergency responder.

"Oh, my baby...please Lord, don't let me lose my baby! I ask you in the name of Jesus Christ to have mercy on his soul. Please God, don't take my baby away from me!" cried out Devell's mother Ms. Barbara Jean.

"Ma'am you have to get back, let us do what we do best, okay!"

"I'm his mother!" said Barbara Jean.

"Okay, I understand that. Could you meet us at the hospital ma'am?" said the emergency responder, as he closed the back of the ambulance, tapping on the wall for the driver to pull off. All you heard was sirens as police cars were just arriving as well as other emergency help like fire trucks and ambulances.

Ms. Barbara Jean ain't have nothing to say as she loaded up her grandkids and took off towards Winter Haven Hospital, praying that they saved her baby boy.

Everybody that witnessed the shooting cooperated with the police, telling them everything, except for the part about Ms. Barbara Jean's son shooting back.

Church people or not, for some reason, they didn't want such a burden on their sister's head.

"Everybody, let's keep sister Hawkins in prayer. The one's who can, let's go to the hospital and show our support." said Pastor Coward as he got his Deacons together and loaded up in the Church vans, heading for Winter Haven Hospital. Knowing that this was a tough situation for Sister Hawkins, he believed in a mighty God, and knew that Sister Hawkins faith was strong as any believers faith could be. "If there was any chance at life for this young man, then it should be!" thought Pastor Coward as he led the caravan of believers to do what they do best, and that was to spread the power of the Holy Spirit.

CHAPTER 12

It didn't take long for the news to spread about the shooting at the church. Everybody and their mammy knew Devell had been gunned down. Some people thought he was dead as others heard he didn't even need medical assistance. They said he had on a bulletproof vest. But everybody that knew better was at the hospital. They had a make shift vigil set up outside, people was praying like Tupac had just been shot. Devell was admired in his community by both the haters and those that had love for him. He always helped people in need no matter who you were; a baser, a cracker, or whoever. He believed in the survival of mankind, some shit he started believing when he was doing time, studying each and every religion. Even though the streets had a strong hold on him, Devell would never take another's life unless he was forced to and had no other choice. But he was far from pussy because he dealt with each and every situation like a true boss supposed to, with an iron fist. That's how he got the respect he had.

Pumpkin kind of already knew what had done took place when she heard it was a black Dodge Challenger on rims that shot Devell up. That's the same car that picked Skeeda up. The same one that crazy ass Damion was driving. She had to call her girl and let her know because no matter what, Tarrell was still her best friend and still would be even after the smoke cleared. The phone ring for about seven times before the answering machine picked up. Pumpkin called her right back, this time Tarrell answered on the third ring.

"Hello!"

"Girl, what are you doing?" asked Pumpkin.

"Nothing bitch, I just got out of the shower. You know I had to scrub you off of my skin. I can't have no signs of you here when my man gets home." said Tarrell.

"Girl, you ain't heard what happened?"

"Heard what bitch?" asked Tarrell with concern in her voice.

"Devell's in the hospital."

"Bitch stop playing with me, what Devell is doing in the hospital?"

"He was shot up, and they say he might not make it...ooooooooohhhh, I'm so sorry Tarrell!"

"Bitch, I ain't got time for all that, I have to get to the hospital. My man needs me!" said Tarrell hanging up the phone, throwing on a pair of Seven denim jeans, a red Cincinnati Reds sweater, and some all-black and red Nike Air Max's. Grabbing her purse and car keys off the counter top, Tarrell raced out the house not even caring about locking up. She jumped in her two door, baby blue BMW 650i and tore out of the drive way, making the little twenty-two inch Forgiatos burn out like a dragster as she raced in and out of traffic at top speeds, heading for the hospital. Not able to think clear at all as thoughts of what her and Pumpkin did must have drove her man to do something crazy.

****

Larry noticed that they had his street taped off like a massacre had occurred, which was true. "But niggas been killing each other like this forever. It's just them crackers always trying to make shit seem worse than what it looks like." thought Old Man Larry as he pulled into his yard next door to Tenille's trap.

"Hey Larry, check it out!" called out baser Poochie, who hung around all the dope boys traps, looking for handouts for his little services like; feeding the dogs, cleaning them, their cars, and running store errands for blunts and shit when they just couldn't go anywhere because the trap was jumping.

"Yea, what is it my man?" asked Larry.

"Be careful over there, I think somebody told the police that you was the one who grabbed them boys out of that house!" said Poochie.

"Damn Pooch, yea! I wonder who would say some shit like that?" Knowing Poochie ass was a compulsive liar, he wasn't at all buying his story. But for drastic measures, Old Man Larry took heed to the warning and told Joann to get in the house. Once they made it inside, he ordered Joann to hurry and wash up and pack a travel bag.

"For what love?" questioned Joann.

"I have to get them boys out of that hospital, and out of

town before any of this shit start running downhill."

"Okay love, I'll be quick!" said Joann as she raced back and forth in the house doing as she was told, ready to ride or die for her man.

Larry went to his wall safe that he had installed in his hall closet, not knowing exactly what it was he had done accumulated over the years. When he opened it, he knew just by looking at the piles of cash, he had enough to do whatever it was he had planned.

Getting one of the Louis Vuitton suit cases out that was also stacked in the same closet, Larry began to neatly stack the bills in, by the bundles, counting as he went. Larry had took a total of three hundred and seventy five thousand dollars, leaving the top shelf still full, just in case something went wrong and he needed a few dollars to fall back on. Grabbing his black gym bag, Larry filled it up with a few pairs of jeans, socks, tee-shirts, sweaters, a jacket, and some boxers. Jumping in the guest bathroom shower, Larry cleaned himself up and got dressed.

"Baby, you want something to eat?" asked Joann. "I can fix you something real quick...."

"Nah baby, we have to get going!" said Larry.

"Okay, I'm ready then." she replied.

"Park the truck in the back yard and pull the van out." ordered Larry, knowing damn well he couldn't ride them boys around in that truck under their conditions. Joann just took off and did what she was asked to do.

Once she brought the van around front, she bumped the horn as she got out to grab her bags. As Larry made it to the van, he placed his bags inside and went back to lock up the house punching in the alarm code. Larry got inside the Ford Econoline 350, taking one last look at Tenille's spot as he noticed the police had done left, but basers ran in and out.

"They must have found a gold mine!" thought Old Man Larry as he saw how big baser Poochie eyes were, knowing he had done been smoking crack nonstop.

Looking over at Joann who now sat in the passenger seat, Old Man Larry put the van in drive and took off. Heading back to Brandon Medical Center, hoping he made it there in time before someone came poking their noses around, preferably the police.

CHAPTER 13

"Momma, what happened?" screamed Tarrell as soon as she spotted Ms. Barbara Jean at the hospital as she waited outside of the E.R. lobby along with what looked like the whole Winter Haven, except it was Pastor Coward and his whole congregation.

"Ohhhh baby!!! Tarrell, they shot my boy right outside the church. They just kept shooting him. Ohhh, what am I going to do without my baby?!" professed Ms. Barbara Jean.

"Do anybody know who did it, momma?" asked Tarrell.

"I don't know child. All I remember seeing was a black car. One of them fancy new ones with them big old rims they be sporting." said Ms. Barbara Jean.

It was like a ton of bricks crashing down on Tarrell. The only person she knew who had a black car that would dare to attempt to get at her man was, Damion Grey.

"But why?" she asked herself, knowing that Devell and Damion was as thick as thieves.

"Momma, are they letting anybody see him yet?"

"Nawl child. He's still in surgery. We don't know if he's even going to make it. They said he would be lucky to survive through the rest of today after all the shots he sustained.

"Don't worry momma! My baby gon' pull through, he's a fighter. Trust me on this, he haven't even began to live yet!" said Tarrell.

"Well baby, I hope you're right! Lord knows I hope you're right." said Ms. Barbara Jean as her mind just drifted off into another land.

"Momma, I'll be right back!" said Tarrell, "I'm just going to step outside for a second to get some fresh air."

"Don't take too long baby, I want as many familiar faces around just in case he comes to. We want to make it as easy as possible."

"Okay momma..." said Tarrell as she rushed out the door, already punching Damion's number in, listening to his phone ring as nobody picked up. Tarrell quickly dialed his number back, getting the same results over and over. Not the one to give up, Tarrell dialed his ass again and Damion finally answered.

"Yea, what's up?" barked Damion, trying to sound demonic as possible, kind of already knowing what it was she was calling him for.

"Damion, what the fuck you did to my man? And don't lie because everybody saw you! Why did you shoot my man?" screamed Tarrell through her phone.

Just like Damion had imagined, he knew the heat was going to fall back on him because of his car. "I just wish that nigga would've told me who it was he had beef with and none of this shit would've ever happened." thought Damion as he did his best to try and explain to Tarrell over the phone.

"Listen to me Tarrell, I didn't shoot Devell. I had no idea what was about to happen!"

"Well who the fuck did it if it wasn't you?" she screamed.

"My lil cousin called me talking about some nigga just tried him and shot his whip up and while we was riding around we passed by this church and it looks like I see my nigga walking up towards my car. So I slow down, but before I could react, Skeeda had rolled the window down talking 'bout; there that fuck nigga go, and started shooting at my nigga, hitting him with round after round. But before Devell went down, he upped his fire and blasted back and caught Skeeda dead in the head, killing him."

"So, you telling me that Skeeda is dead?" asked Tarrell.

"Hell yea, as dead as a door knob. I dumped his ass out about two blocks away and kept it tight." said Damion.

"So, where you at right now?"

"Come on Tarrell! You know I ain't going out like that!"

"Ole bitch ass nigga, you going out some kind of way! You better hope my man make it, because if he don't I swear to you I'll kill you." promised Tarrell as she listened to Damion bark back his own threats.

"Bitch, I wish you would even attempt to harm me. I'll cut your fuck ass up into little pieces and eat you for dinner. I told you I didn't do it, but since you seem not to understand that, then fuck you and fuck that nigga. I don't give a damn if he live or die!" threatened Damion, all in his feelings.

Tarrell just hung up, knowing how dangerous Damion were. She couldn't fuck up and cause any more harm than what was already done. That's when she strolled through her cell phone's phone book and looked up his number. Devell had always warned her to only use the number in case of an emergency as she pressed the call button, sending the call all the way through to Devell's best friend, and the only person he trusted with his life.

"Hello, who am I speaking to?" said the voice on the other end of the phone before Tarrell could even speak.

"I'm sorry for calling like this, but it's Devell!"

"Why, what's wrong with him?"

"He was shot today leaving church and he's in the hospital undergoing surgery right now." said Tarrell.

"Where you at right now?" he asked.

"I'm at the hospital right now."

"Is his momma there, or do she even know?"

"Yea, she's here. Everybody is here." said Tarrell, hoping to lift up Devell's best friend spirit just in case the news of him being shot was too much for him to bear. But not knowing that the person on the other end of the phone wasn't easily moved, he got off on two things only. That's murder, and money.

Whatever situation called for his services, let's just say you wouldn't want him coming after you because there was no place on earth that could hide you when your name came up.

"Listen to me carefully, tell no one that you have talked to me. Devell must have trusted you a lot to give you this number! But be assured, whoever played a part in him being shot up will be dealt with." he said calmly, but in a more severe manner. "I'll be there shortly, so be expecting my arrival. I must go for now." was the last words Tarrell heard as the call ended.

All she was able to think about was the demeanor in his voice, how authorative it was, hoping he came and punished Damion for what he did, knowing he was probably the one who shot Devell. "Even when he use to make all them slick remarks because I wouldn't never fuck with him." thought Tarrell to herself as she headed back inside the hospital.

****

Just the thought of his main man dying on him had King George in a rage as he kicked a leg off the dining table in his New York City condo. "If only his nigga would have been left that small ass city! I been told him Winter

Haven didn't have shit to offer him except one of the Florida prison cells, or a plot at one of them grave yards." Now he done let a nigga catch him slippin' and gunned him down. "I bet old Ms. Barbara Jean is going crazy!" he thought as he realized it was somebody who actually cared about his nigga more than what he did.

Notifying all his people, he told them that he would be away for a while but to keep business going as usual until they heard otherwise from him. Packing a few personal belongings, King George grabbed a titanium special designed suitcase that contained the most sensitive explosive equipment known to man. He also grabbed his Gucci tote bag and filled it up with money from his safe, knowing what he was about to do, he couldn't afford to use any of his credit cards that would leave traceable evidence. Calling his personal driver, he told him to get ready, he'd be down front in five minutes.

"Okay boss!" said Otis, who was his personal driver as well as body guard and child-hood friend.

"Let me see what the fuck this nigga done got himself into. And no matter what, I'm bringing my nigga back with me." he thought as he headed out of his condo for Florida." A place that he had put way behind himself, for reasons he only had the answers to. "It's amazing how you can re-live your past all over again!"

CHAPTER 14

Officer Fulwiley had made it to the holding tank where Moneisha was just in time as he heard over his walkie-talkie for an officer to deliver the detainee to Detective Grant on B-wing. Officer Fulwiley knew right then that Detective Grant meant to fuck her around, so he hurried up and rushed her to where her sister was, in a more secure environment.

"Oh my God Chi-Chi, what happened to you?" asked her twin as she looked up at her sister's eye and mouth all busted up.

"That detective dude got pissed I didn't tell him shit!" said Chineir, still looking like the bad bitch she was, busted up and all.

"Damn sis, I'm so sorry. I wish that I would have listened to you when you told me that; all money wasn't good money. But when them niggas started talking about them stacks, you already know me girl!" laughed Moneisha.

"Yea, I know your hot ass. That's exactly why I came. I'm not about to let anyone fuck over my baby sister!"

"You mean big sister!" replied Moneisha.

"Whatever girl, you know I was born four and a half minutes before you!" said Chineir.

"Anyways bitch! Come here!" said Moneisha as she grabbed her sister and wrapped her up in her embrace while officer Fulwiley just looked at them, trying to figure out a way to get these two bad bitches up out of there.

"I want the both of you to do exactly as I say and I'll get you up out of here. Don't go anywhere with anybody except me. Even if you have to kick and fight, you better do it as if your life depended on it. You're safe right here because of the heavy surveillance. But trust me, everywhere in here is not safe..."

"You tell me about it!" remarked Chineir.

"I should be gone for only a few minutes and we're out of here." said Officer Fulwiley.

"Thank you so much, Mr. Police Man!"

"Yea, thank you!" added Chineir, following her sister as they both put on their puppy faces, knowing they were the best at it, especially how they pouted their lips.

"What the fuck am I doing?" thought Officer Fulwiley. "I could end up in jail for what I'm about to do! Fuck it, It's not like I'm a fucking saint anyways. Plus, I can always use this as part of the investigation knowing the D.A. wanted Homicide Detective Gerry Grant with a passion. Checking the get-a-way route he was planning on using, Officer Fulwiley made sure the coast was clear for the loading dock where the police usually came and went when transporting detainees.

Officer Fulwiley went and got his personal car, a 2009 all black Dodge Charger, black factory rims and tires.

There was nothing special about it except it was paid for. Once he pulled it inside the loading dock, he quickly made it back to the holding tank where the twins were undetected. It was crazy how the precinct was and still nobody had a clue to what was about to happen.

"Y'all ready?" asked Officer Fulwiley, getting nods of approval from them both as they hurried up and rushed the door.

"Y'all hold the fuck up, you muthafuckas about to get all of our asses fucked up moving like that!" said Officer Fulwiley.

"I'm sorry!" apologized Moneisha, ready to get the fuck out of there.

"I'm sorry too!" said Chineir, apologizing as well as they crept slowly behind the cop determined to make it out of that place alive.

"When we get to the end of this hallway, we're going to make a left and my car is parked right outside the door. Both of you need to get in the back seat and duck down because there's cameras everywhere outside of this place."

The twins just followed orders and kept the chatter to a minimum. Moneisha was willing to do anything for this police officer at the moment; hell, he was putting his own life on the line just to help us. That shit meant a lot to her she thought as they made it to his car. As soon as he opened the door, they noticed the car was parked so close to the door that you would think they were about to transfer some serial killer.

Once they were in the back seat and ducked down for cover, another officer came running up.

"Hey Fulwiley, how about them Miami Heat?" asked Officer Hernandez, who was a transfer from Miami-Dade P.D.

"Fuck them Heat! You know I'm a Spur till I die!" replied Officer Fulwiley.

"Yea, yea, yea! You just saying that because y'all just won the Championship. You wasn't saying none of that last year!" barked back Officer Hernandez.

"Whatever man, y'all ain't give us shit! We took that from y'all. It isn't our fault that Pop sat Tim Duncan in the last seconds of the game."

"Alright, you got that. I'm going to halla at you later. I have to get out of here right now. My sister done came up missing again and she left the kids at home all by themselves with nothing to eat." lied Officer Fulwiley, knowing anybody that was familiar with him or his family knew his sister had a drug problem and wouldn't believe anything he said when it came to such an issue.

"Alright then, just make sure to halla at me. Are we still on for this weekend or not? You know I'm new around here and need your help pal!" said Hernandez.

"You damn right we still on, you just better be ready because I'm taking you out in the jungle this time around."

"What you mean you're taking me in the jungle?"

"It's this club that's owned by this former drug kingpin called; Club Conversations. It's rated the number one spot in Central Florida." said Officer Fulwiley.

"Naw! I'll past on that kind of crowd. I'm not trying to get killed just for asking a beautiful lady what's her name!"

stated Officer Hernandez.

"Trust me, this ain't that type of spot. This club is for the grown and sexy, and them big ballers. And besides, I like how this owner operate his club. It's zero tolerance when it comes to violence, so you know what that mean?"

"You damn right I do. Count me in!" said Hernandez as he gave Fulwiley a fist pound.

"Hey, when you catch up with your sister, try to take it easy with her okay. She'll get better in time."

"Bet that up. We'll, I'm on my way. I'll halla back at you later." said Officer Fulwiley as he waited on Officer Hernandez to leave his presence before getting into his car.

Once he made it inside, Officer Fulwiley hurried up and got in his car, peeking into the back seat to make sure his precious cargo was still there.

"Y'all okay?" asked Officer Fulwiley.

"Just go, please...I'm scared!" stated Chineir, not wanting to ever come face to face with that Detective again, especially after he tried to squeeze the life out of her.

"So, where y'all from?"

"Tampa," offered Moneisha, hoping he didn't mind taking them all the way home She thought as Chi-Chi shot her a sharp elbow to the mid-section for talking too much.

"What was that for?" whispered Moneisha.

"You talk too much. Why tell him where we're from? He might be tricking us." said Chineir.

"Come on sis, they got our finger prints and all. How is we going to hide from that?"

"I didn't think about that. I'm just tripping Moe! I'm

just trying to get away from these fake ass cops. They're just as bad as us."

"I know sis, but we don't have any time to waste. If he's going to help, which he's already showed that, then we have to take advantage of that and pray we make it home safe."

"Okay...and thanks a lot!" said Chineir.

"Thanks for what?" Moe asked, hoping her twin wasn't about to melt down on her in the back seat of this officer's car.

"For always being there at my side. Even when I'm stuck on that bullshit, you never turned your back on me or told me no, and I love you for that." Confessed Chineir.

"That's what I'm here for, you're my twin sister! Hell, what would I do without you?"

"Hey, you know I can hear you two back there!" said Officer Fulwiley.

"Oh, we're sorry." said Chineir, apologizing for her and her sister.

"It's okay. But for future references, y'all need to try and choose the things y'all talk about more wisely, especially in the back seat of the police car."

"What do you mean by that? We didn't say anything wrong, and we didn't do nothing." pleaded Moneisha.

"Yea, you're right. But I'm not talking about that right now. I'm talking about when I was bringing y'all to the station in my police cruiser. It was a sensitive recording microphone system that will pick up a fly's fart." Said Officer Fulwiley.

"So what do that have to do with us?" Asked Chineir.

"I don't know, but you tell me who the hell Odell is?" Asked Officer Fulwiley, bringing shock and disbelief to their faces as tears began to flow down the cheeks of both their faces.

"We didn't know, you have to believe us, all we can admit to you is that we was gon' try to set these niggas up who came to our job where we dance at, throwing money and making it rain. So, we hit up our cousin Odell and GPS tagged our phones for him to know where we were and the last thing we remembered was that we was about to come out and perform for these niggas, and that's when gun shots just started to ring out and seemed like it would never stop. We hid in the closet and didn't come out until you showed up and that's exactly how it went." Confessed Moneisha hoping they didn't fuck up by talking too much.

"I'm just going to let it play by ear, but I'm letting both of y'all know that you owe me and I'm telling y'all right now that I'm going to get what's owed to me!" stated Officer Fulwiley.

"Man, whatever you want, I promise you we got you. All you have to do is say it. But don't put those murders on us." said Chineir, knowing she would kill herself before she went to one of those prisons.

But officer Fulwiley had something in store for both of their ass. He imagined that they thought he probably wanted to fuck, which he did, but that wasn't the importance at the moment. He cracked a smile out the side of his mouth as he jumped on the Polk Parkway, heading towards Tampa knowing now that he had somebody to push the drugs on that he had cuffed at the crime scene.

****

"Hey there Officer Hernandez!" spoke Detective Grant. "Have you seen Fulwiley anywhere?" he asked.

"I just seen him heading out, said something about his sister had went missing and the kids was home alone."

"Was there anybody with him?"

"As I recall, he was by himself." thought Officer Hernandez as he tried to remember whether or not was there anyone with Fulwiley.

"I'm certain he was alone!" stated Officer Hernandez, finally coming to his senses realizing he had held a brief conversation with him before he came to work, and his car was parked right at the door.

"Damn, this is some crazy shit. How in the fuck these hoes just disappear out of thin air and don't nobody know where in the fuck they went." thought Detective Grant. "Something ain't right, and I'm going to get to the bottom of it. Ain't no way the only suspects to a triple murder going to just walk out of my police station and don't nobody know shit!"

Detective Grant went furious as he ordered everybody to gather around for one of his menacing speeches as he threatened the whole police force if they didn't tell him something, and he meant something right now.

Chapter 15

Tarrell was trying to console her mother-in-law, when in fact, she couldn't control herself. She was an emotional wreck, all that she could think about was; this was all my fault! If she wouldn't have never tried her man the way she did! But how could she have known that Devell would be against her and her sexual preference. "Every woman thought that it was a man's dream to have two women in the bed at the same time, especially if one of the women is the ol' lady!" At least that's what Tarrell thought, but now she was beating herself up about it because her man was fighting for his own life because of her sexual desires.

Sitting in the waiting area along with Devell's family, their friends, and the church members who had refused to leave until their God showed up and revealed His power. So, in reality, it was a hot mess in there. Tarrell tried to relax as her and Ms. Barbara Jean kind of leaned in on one another's body trying to embrace themselves from slumping over and falling asleep. Her phone began to vibrate. She didn't have her ringer off so she knew it had to either the battery was about to die, or a text message. Taking the phone out of her pocket, she seen there was a text from the same forbidden number that Devell had given her and warned her only to use in case of an emergency. She pulled it up on the touch screen and swiped the message up. It read: Send me all the names of the people who was involved with this. Everybody they're affiliated with, as well as their numbers and addresses if you have any of that information.

Tarrell kind of knew by the sound of that text what was about to happen. Usually she would be against the violence, especially if it caused for her to participate in it. But she also knew that this was all her fault and she wanted to help make it right, and if giving this mystery man all the information she had, then that's exactly what she was about to do. Even Pumpkin's information because she had to know something. And besides, it was her man that shot Devell so it was whatever, she was ready to represent for her man.

Sitting there in that waiting room, Tarrell couldn't help but think about all the what-if's. She had done sent him everything she had. All the names, the possibilities, and all. But, was beginning to feel bad now, like she was betraying her best friend. Somebody she'd shared her whole life with. She knew that she couldn't stop what was about to happen. All she could do was pray and hope nothing happened to Pumpkin, realizing she truly loved her. Tarrell made a promise to herself that if Pumpkin was killed because of her, she would take her own life. Even though she loved Devell, she couldn't live without Pumpkin; the real love of her life.

****

The private jet had landed over an hour ago, King George had went over detail by detail exactly what had to be done. He made sure that he addressed it clearly to his body guard Big-O the seriousness of this mission and the zero room for any error. Big-O was certified, and was willing to put whatever work in that was necessary for his boss. Truth is, their relationship went a lot deeper than just business. Big-O grew up alongside Devell and King George as well. He just didn't have the knack for the business side of the game and what all it took to lead others. Every time the opportunity presented itself for him, he would always find ways to fuck it up. Big-O was a professional thief. That was his hustle of passion, and he was good at it. That stealing shit always rubbed everyone he fucked with the wrong way and made it hard for them to fuck with him because it was hard to trust a thief. But, with Devell and King George things was totally different. They knew clearly what their big homie was capable of, and they used it to their strengths, keeping him close and making sure he was straight as far as money and living the life most people could only dream of.

King George had just went over the text message he received back from Tarrell and went over its content thoroughly with Big-O, sharing the same info with him as they decided on what leads to take. King George chose to get the nigga Damion, the lil young bitch he fuck with in St. Paul, and his baby momma, some chick name Bookie from Winter Haven. Where Big-O was going by this nigga Skeeda's house and pay whoever there an unexpected visit. Even though the nigga was slumped, when a nigga got out of line, you always have to get at their family because it sent a message to all of the other wanna-be-thugs and gangstas that if you try your hand and failed, this is what the results will be. Big-O crunk up the massive S.U.V. that King George kept in the garage at the airport hangar. It had been sitting there now for over three years, that was the last time he had to make this trip back to his home town.

Hearing the big powerful engine of the military grade Humvee roar to life, he knew he was ready. This was King George's favorite vehicle. It was equipped with everything. He had purchased it at a private auction in Tampa, Florida, where the late Colonel Willie M. Miller whole estate was being auctioned off. Colonel Miller was an intelligence specialist with the United States Marines and this Humvee was the exact same one that was used in the Desert Storm over in Iraq. the only thing different was the color. It was painted matte black all over, with limo tint that set the Humvee off just right. It still had the high intelligence media system, equipped with Global Positioning Surveillance with access to military, Federal, and all State records. So, if you had a name, social, or even a phone number, you could be tracked down which is what being used at this very moment as he tried to locate the whereabouts of this nigga Damion Grey, whose car was supposedly used in the shooting.

They found no physical address on Damion, but it still showed his mug shot for both State and Federal prisons. Displayed his driver's license, as well as his car and every piece of personal information available for him. King George hit the vehicle search for Damion's car and after a few quick spins it was displayed on the monitor. A 2015 all black Dodge Challenger. Its current real time location showed Panama City, Florida. King George put the phone number that Tarrell had given him into the computers system for most activity search and it displayed two numbers that has been frequently used over twenty times each in the past 48 hours. This system was so advanced, even though it was an old one, it was something the world would never get to experience, at least the general population. King George hit profile section to see what all it had on the two numbers, and the first one; 863-288-0101 which belonged to a 'Asia Dominique' popped up her photo, her address, and her current employer which read high school student.

"Damn, lil momma cute!" stated King George.

"Yea! Let me check her out." asked Big-O, looking at the screens display after it was positioned in his direction.

"Yea, you right! That bitch damn sho' is tuff. I'll do something awful to that there!" said Big-O as he chuckled along with his main man and boss at the comment he just made.

"Boy you're crazy. But we will pay her a visit, and if lil momma is stank with it, then we'll show her how real niggas treat outsiders." said King George.

"Now I'm with that! So where to now?" asked Big-O.

"Let's take it to the hospital. I have to see what's going on with my nigga and let Ms. Barbara Jean see my face, because I know it will break her heart if she found out I was in town and didn't come by to check on her."

"Yea Big Homie, you're right about that. We have a few people to stop by and check out!" said Big-O, throwing it out there in the air because he damn sho' wanted to see his baby momma. It's been a while. Being in New York and always on the road with King George kept Big-O out of touch with almost everyone he loved.

"Yea, we'll try to get at everybody. Let's get at this situation at hand for the moment!" said King George as he continued to check up on all the leads, retrieving all the info he could get about everyone, because any one of them could be responsible for my nigga being laid up in the hospital he thought.

The Twins, Moneisha and Chineir looking as sexy as any bad bitch can.

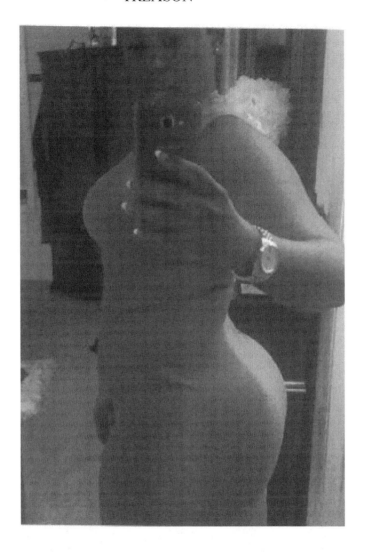

Damion's young bitch, Asia. A six-foot two, sixteen year old Amazon.

Damion's menacing Dodge Challenger on 26'
Forgiatos

The 2 door Cadillac on 28' D.U.B. spinners that
Skeeda gave Pumpkin.

Devell's main bitch, Tarrell and Skeeda's bitch Pumpkin. Their forbidden love affair is what caused the demise of their lives.

The Notorious gangsta, Damion. They say a picture is worth a thousand words.

The Humvee that King George purchased from retired

Colonel Willie M .Miller. It was used to track down everyone who had something to do with Devell's shooting.

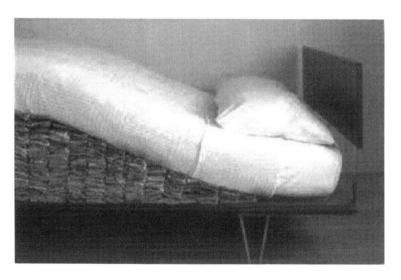

The money Big-O cuffed when he killed Skeeda's bitch
Pumpkin.

The animal bitch, Pharah who used the juices from her pussy to seal the blunt she smoked with Odell.

Odell's Infinity S.U.V. on 32' Forgiatos

Odell's business partner, Vent posted in front of his Buick Lacross on 32' D.U. B. Spinners.

Chapter 16

Pumpkin was still mad at the fact that Skeeda never gave her the combination to his safe. But she wasn't about to let none of that stop her from getting inside of it. She had done called Skeeda's best friend, a nigga name 'N'. Him and Skeeda was stacking that paper together, especially 'N', he never spent his money. Pumpkin always beat herself up about choosing Skeeda instead of 'N', but how would she have known that 'N' was holding the way he was.

Her quick plan turned to genius because that lil episode with Tarrell's nigga was all she needed to get Skeeda dumb ass to jump out there like he ain't have any sense. He fell for it too, especially when she told his ass; When he found out that was your car, he shot it up. Not wanting to seem pussy, he called his cousin Damion, making the biggest mistake in his life, one that would cost him his own life.

Pumpkin had done packed up everything. She had hit the jackpot with Skeeda's jewelry. He had a bunch of sets, and all of his shit was iced out. He had well over two hundred grand worth, she had made him get most of it when they would hit up the shops. She knew he was a busta, so she tried him on every corner. Then one day he begged her to move in. As much as Pumpkin tried not to accept his proposal, she couldn't get over the thought of Skeeda promising to take care of her, everything on him. Unfortunately, Skeeda managed to get her pregnant three times, and each time Pumpkin would devilishly do something awful to kill the baby that was growing inside of her womb.

The last pregnancy she had swallowed a mouthwash cap full of Clorox bleach that almost killed her as well. They had to rush her to the hospital and pump the chemical out of her system. Skeeda found out she was murdering their unborn seeds. He tried to despise her, but he couldn't find the strength to leave her. Pumpkin was a bad bitch and Skeeda was still madly in love with her. But lately, he had stopped breaking bread with her the way he use to and Pumpkin knew it, she knew this nigga was acting funny and wasn't about to let another bitch eat her plate.

She had done packed all the luggage she was taking with her into the all-black two-door Cadillac CTS-V Skeeda had bought her for her birthday. All she was waiting on now was 'N' to come through and bust this safe open so she can hit the highway. Pumpkin was going straight to Atlanta and start all over.

About to head back into the house, 'N' came pulling up in an old ass 1800's looking truck bumping the horn. Pumpkin just shook her head at the thought of this cheap ass nigga as she turned around to meet him in the driveway. 'N' got out of the truck and came walking up as he looked inside the CTS.

"Look like y'all about to go on a lil vacation!" said 'N' dead to the fact that Skeeda had been killed. Even though they were partners, 'N' was from Bartow, but lived in the Inwood area. He wasn't social, and nobody even knew about Skeeda's death except the ones it was told to. 'N' didn't even know about the nigga Devell being blasted. But it was all over Facebook and in the streets already and it hasn't been twenty-four hours yet.

"So, what's up with you Pumpkin. What's the emergency you need me for?" asked 'N'.

"I need you to bust this safe open for me!"

"What safe?" he asked.

"Skeeda's safe." Pumpkin said hoping this nigga didn't bitch up on her.

"Why you just don't get him to do it himself?" asked 'N'.

"Because he won't, and besides, he's not coming back." stated Pumpkin.

"What you mean he's not coming back? Where the fuck my nigga at?" asked 'N' because she was sounding like my man had done got cased up or something.

"He got some other bitch! I caught them together and we had a big ass fight and I came here and packed my shit up, and I'm going to take all of his money with me. Fuck that nigga 'N', he don't like you either. He always talking bad about you!" said Pumpkin.

'N' wasn't about to feed into Pumpkin's emotional roller coaster because he knew first-hand about how them hoes get all emotional and shit when they wanted to burn a nigga up, especially right now. This bitch was trying to hit Skeeda for all of his paper. 'N' knew Skeeda was caked up and for real, he wondered how much paper his nigga had himself.

"So, what's in it for me?" asked 'N' trying to get something out of the deal.

Pumpkin paused for a moment, she knew this was her only chance to get this safe open.

"Okay, I'll give you half. Just get it open!" begged Pumpkin, bringing an evil smile to 'N's face.

"I'll be right back. I have to grab something off the truck!" he said.

"You need to hurry up, I don't have all day. I'm trying to get the fuck out of here." screamed Pumpkin.

It didn't take 'N' two minutes to get what he was looking for as he grabbed the gas operated brick cutter. 'N' replaced the diamond blade that he usually used when he did construction; a little business he operated to cover up his illegal activities. 'N' replaced the blade with the carbide blade. This blade specialized in cutting through steel, or any kind of reinforcement. When he made it back into the house Pumpkin knew he meant business. Just the look at the saw made her think this was his profession.

"Let's go!" said 'N' "Where the fuck is this safe at?" he asked, not believing he was about to take half of his main man's paper. That show you when it came to that almighty dollar, a nigga would take from his own momma.

Pumpkin led 'N' to the massive floor to ceiling safe in the hallway that Skeeda had professionally installed. As soon as 'N' recognized it, it was a Wells Fargo double breasted cage safe. He knew once you opened the first door, it was another combination style turnkey lock that you had to get past to get inside. 'N' went straight to work. He dropped the all-black shades he had resting on top of his head down over his eyes for protection and crunk the powerful saw up. He sawed away at the steel brackets that held the doors on. The carbide blade sliced through the six inch diameter steel bars like a hot butter knife to butter.

'N' still had a ways to go. Normally, any of those regular safe's, once you sliced through the door handles the door would fall off. But with this Wells Fargo safe, the inside combination had a fan lock that connected into place on three quarters of the safe's gateway that was fireproof padded. 'N' used the saw's carbide blade to slice through the three security locks and then used the size thirteen Timberland boots he had on to kick the extra door off. After about seven mule kicks, the door fell face down. 'N' couldn't believe what he was seeing. Ain't no way in hell Skeeda was holding this much cash. 'N' didn't have a fraction of what he was seeing. It was at least a few million dollars that he was witnessing.

'N' grabbed a stack of bills and held them up to the light, knowing all this money had to be fake. But, 'N' seen that his theory was wrong. All this money was real, and 'N' wanted his half. He wanted his right now. He wanted it all, and he was going to take it all right now. *"FUCK THIS BITCH! SHE DON'T DESERVE NONE OF IT. SHE WANTED TO STEAL IT."* thought 'N' as he quickly thought of how he was going to remove all this money from this humongous safe...*"Garbage bags!"* he thought as he realized that would be the best way to get all of the money from point A to point B. 'N' looked around and Pumpkin wasn't anywhere in sight, she had to think he was still trying to get the safe open. But little did she know the safe was already open and what she wanted so badly was about to disappear before she was even able to witness it.

'N' seen it was a bathroom right beside the safe and knew it had to be some garbage bags in there. After plundering around for about ten seconds, he found just what he was looking for, a box of heavy duty trash bags. 'N' grabbed two of them, just in case he needed some extra support. He ain't need shit busting on him as he tried to get away. Coming out of the bathroom with the bags in his hand, not paying attention to his surroundings as he tried to pop the garbage bag open, he caught a glimpse of the sharp object that illuminated above his peripheral that made him look up as Pumpkin was coming down with the ax using all of her force, catching 'N' in the center of his head, splitting his skull in half as the ax laid stuck there.

'N' couldn't even react to the ax as he got caught up like a deer in some headlights. His greed made him lose his focus, something he never before allowed himself to do. *"But this time it was different, she was a woman and it should have been easy."* was some of the thoughts that flooded his mind as his body crashed to the floor, sending a pool of blood everywhere.

Pumpkin grabbed the bags that was still gripped inside 'N's hand, tearing them away as she filled the bags up with all the money from the safe. It was so much money

Pumpkin couldn't believe it herself...*"She was rich!"* was all she could think of as she took away every single bill off each shelf, trying to hurry up and get the fuck out of town.

"Ain't no way in hell I'm going to let somebody take any of this from me!" she said to herself as she raced back and forth with the first bag of money, stuffing it inside her car as she raced back inside for the next, not seeing the all-black Humvee as it pulled up in the driveway.

Chapter 17

As the two corporate looking thugs marched into Winter Haven's Medical Center where Devell was being treated at, they unintentionally stole everyone's stares as the remaining Church members that were still lingering around in support of Devell's mother, their Church sister, Ms. Barbara Jean even wondered if they were the attackers from earlier.

Just looking at the two men brung chills to your body. Their eyes, it was something wrong about the glare they displayed, like it wasn't any life there. Still though, their appearance was immaculate as Big-O wore a burnt orange, pin stripe custom made suit by Deep Vision Italian collection. A pair of burnt brown Deep Vision hard bottom loafers, with a soft brown turtle neck sweater that was made by Deep Vision as well. Big-O rocked a bald head that he kept super clean and shiny at all times, with an oversized Rick Ross beard that was trimmed to perfection. If you didn't know any better, you'd think he was a Muslim. Even though Big-O had a baby face, his six foot four inch, three hundred pound frame told a totally different story than the baby face he presented. And Big-O never once had a problem when it came to demonstrating his many violent physical talents.

Now King George was made up a little different. He was only six foot two, two hundred and thirty pounds. But his bite was a lot harder. He specialized in torture and murder. He never missed a target. Being that they were coming from New York, their attire were different. Even though it was mid-November, the weather in New York to Florida was totally the opposite and King George knew it, unlike Big-O.

He wore a white, tailor made linen suit, white soft loafers, and a white silk V-neck all by Ro'Mi Wear. He was neatly trimmed, with the thin manicured beard that covered his jaw line, mustache, and chin. Except, he kept his chin hairs long and rugged looking. He wore the hair on his head cut in a Cesar, displaying a head full of waves. He also had a mouthful of gold teeth, the whole thirty-two done in rose gold, diamonds, and rubies. When it came to stuntin', King George didn't short himself at all. He felt he worked too hard to get where he was and happy-damn if he was going to leave it behind for someone else to fuck it up.

When Ms. Barbara Jean turned around to see what all the fuss and whispers were about, she almost fainted when noticed the two men that appeared. King George was like a second son of hers. She hated when he had left because when he was around she knew Devell was gon' be alright.

"It's been what! Almost nine years now?" She to whispered to King George as she gave him a motherly hug that said so much. But the main thing it said was; I'm glad you're here now. And even though she lived for God, it was something's that could take you away from doing what was right, and trying to kill her baby boy was one of them. Deep down in her head, she hoped and wished with all her might that whoever was responsible got exactly what he deserved.

"Hey there momma?" said King George as he tried to read Ms. Barbara Jean's body language, hoping the worst haven't happened.

"I'm so glad to see you, please do something for my baby, you always know what to do!" stressed Ms. Barbara Jean as she released herself from their hug looking him in the eyes, showing her desperation.

"Yea, I'm here now, and everything's going to be alright!" King George assured as he continued to talk. "So, what's up, how is he doing? Have they told you anything yet?"

"Baby, they haven't told me anything yet." replied Ms. Barbara Jean as the sadness that covered her face made her look as if she had aged twenty years older in the ten hours since they were at the hospital.

"You just relax and I'll go and check to see what's up with bro, okay! I'll be right back." said King George as he approached the doctors that stood about twenty feet away. Big-O stayed back because he didn't know whether or not the threat was on Devell's family or just him. He was going to make sure as long as he was around that Ms. Barbara Jean was protected.

As King George made it up to the doctors, he politely interrupted them.

"Excuse me! May I ask who is the senior Doctor or nurse in charge of this shift?"

"Well, that would be me!" stated the tall, slender black man that looked to be no older than thirty.

"I hope this nigga ain't the one responsible for fixing bro up!" thought King George as he spoke to the man who claimed he was in charge.

"I would like to know the status on the patient who came in earlier with the multiple gunshot wounds. Is he okay, stable, unstable, dead, or in a coma? My family has been waiting over there patiently and not once did anybody give them an update on his current condition."

The Doctor didn't even know how to come back with a response because he knew this person who was checking him was correct.

"Sir, I'm sorry to be an inconvenience, and I deeply apologize for the lack of unprofessionalism that me and my staff has presented. This is a mere misunderstanding and I assure you that this will not happen again. Now if you don't mind me asking, what is the patient's name sir?" asked the Doctor, as he did his best to try and talk over King George's head, thinking by his appearance that he was just another street dummy. He was highly educated, but chose the street life for his heart will always be dedicated to them. The streets is what raised him.

"His name is Devell Hawkins!"

"Yes, I'm aware of the patient's condition. We were under the impression that there was no family here for him!" said the Doctor.

"What? You mean to tell me that y'all actually believed, or actually think that I'm going to believe that y'all didn't know he had family out here?" said King George in an angry tone.

The Doctor saw that he couldn't shoot just any bullshit over this man's head as he tried to dig himself out of the hole he was stuck in.

"So, what is your relation to the patient sir? Are you immediately family?" asked the Doctor as he saw the squint appear in the man's eyes. He knew that he had done fucked up.

"Let me tell your wannabe, highly educated ass a few words of advice...'If that patient in there don't make it, then you don't make it.' And trust me Doc, I'm a man of my word." barked King George at the Doctor not knowing he almost made him shit on himself.

Trembling, the doctor begin to speak through stuttered words. Never in his life have he been threatened, and never in his life would he have imagined he would be threatened at his job for doing what he was trained to do.

"I think you made yourself loud and clear, sir. Like I said before, I apologize and I'll get on top of that immediately. Now, may I excuse myself, I have a patient to make sure his life is saved!" said the Doctor as he asked the menacing man's permission.

Wanting to slap the shit out of this clown ass nigga who so-called himself a Doctor, King George nodded his head, giving the Doctor permission to go, but for two reasons and two reasons only; the first being that Ms.

Barbara Jean was there and he always respected her regardless of the fact she knew what it was they all did for a living. And secondly, his main man Devell, his safety and well-being meant the world right now and he needed this Doctor to do whatever it took to make all that a reality.

Going back to where Ms. Barbara Jean was, she didn't waste any time as she asked about her baby boy. "What did they say about my son?" she pleaded.

"When that Doctor come back out, I promise you Ma that he'll bring us some good news, okay! So cheer up..." said King George trying to comfort Ms. Barbara Jean as much as possible.

"Hey Ma, who is that chick Big-O is talking to?" asked King George, wondering what the fuck they had in common to be laughing and carrying on.

"That's Tarrell, she's your brother's ol' lady."

"Yea, that's how bro rolling?" said King George to himself as he tried to examine the chick who was supposed to be holding Devell down. She wasn't ugly, but she damn sho' wasn't pretty. As he headed towards them he was able to tell she had some pretty ass eyes. But the more she talked, he was able to see that big ass gap in her mouth, which was totally unattractive. She was tall and kind of slim, that's the way he remembered Devell liking them...with a little booty. But this chick ain't have no ass at all. It looked like she tried to wear her pants in a sag, like a nigga on the block. *"This shit have to stop!"* thought King George as he made his presence known.

"So, what's up? What y'all got going on over here?" he asked, wondering what the fuck these muthafuckas could be whispering about when his main man's life was on the line.

"Nothing much boss. I was just trying to feel lil momma out and see what she knows." said Big-O.

"I was just telling him about the way all of this went down." Said Tarrell.

"Oh yea! And how did it all go down?" asked King George as he gave his full attention, because if this bitch knew something then she should've mentioned it over the phone.

"I was just telling him how I tried to surprise Devell with a threesome. But when he came home, he snapped and rushed out of the house and shot the girl car up."

"Who car? What girl?" asked King George.

"Pumpkin!"

"You mean the same bitch who nigga you said shot my boy?"

"Yea, that's the same one!" answered Tarrell, hoping she didn't place Pumpkin in any trouble.

"Alright, I guess I do have to pay this bitch a visit. I was going to try and leave the love ones out of this, but this shit just don't sound right." mumbled King George quietly, but loud enough to be heard by only Big-O and his main man's broad.

"You want me to go and handle that?" asked Big-O as he offered his services. Tarrell had showed him a picture of her and the bitch was bad as far as face and body went. Well, bad enough for Big-O's standards, and he had something in store for the bitch. All King George had to do was say the word and it was on and poppin.

Knowing what had to be done, he had no other choice but to let Big-O handle this mission alone, however he wanted to. He still had to make sure everything was straight at the hospital before he left. He wasn't about to let the doctor get off the hook so easily. And besides, if my nigga didn't make it, I was gon' make sure that Doc' knew I was a man of my word thought King George as he put together a master plan for this trick bitch Pumpkin.

"Don't play no games. Hit this bitch quick and hard then get back to me. I'm going to be here with Ms. Barbara Jean for a while to see how bro pulls through. If anything changes I'll fill you in."

"Okay Boss. This shouldn't take no time. I'll hit you up as soon as I'm up out of there." Big-O said as he gave King George some pound with his fist and cutting out the side of his eye at Tarrell as he turned around and headed out of the hospital to the Humvee.

"Everybody that had something to do with my nigga getting shot up, I'm killing them. I hope at the end of the day your name will be cleared! But, if not! I'm going to personally fuck you over." threatened King George as he stared coldly at Tarrell, letting her know he was serious and that he didn't give a fuck about her being his main man's bitch. Hoes came a dime a dozen, and once he got Devell up to New York with him, he knew he'd find him a real down ass bitch that would be able to represent and hold a real nigga down. "I gotta get bro out of Florida before one of these sucka ass niggas take his life."

Chapter 18

After Officer Fulwiley dropped Moneisha and Chineir off in some gated community in the Palm River area. A small community called 'Green Ridge Estates'. He had exchanged numbers and all other personal information he needed to contact the twins, including their cousin Odell's number who they implicated that could possibly be the murderer.

"I'll be back!" was the last thing that Officer Fulwiley had said to the twins as he pushed his all black Dodge Charger back out of the gated community.

Odell had came out to greet his cousins because he was worried sick about them. He haven't heard from them since they sent him the GPS, tagging his phone.

"Unn unn bitch! Bring your ass inside the house, I know you ain't even try us like this, cuz!" said Moneisha, like she would to a bitch in the streets that she was about to put her hands on.

"What the fuck is you talking about?" asked Odell as he knew something was wrong by the way Chineir was crying as he paid close attention to the black eye she was wearing hoping them fuck niggas they slid from their job with didn't rape his lil cousin, because if they did he was ready to suit up and put his chopper on them fuck niggas.

"Cuz, stop playing dumb, nigga! You came up in them boys spot and killed them...you killed them cuz, for what?" creamed Moe.

"You got me fucked up. I ain't kill no fucking body. I'm still fucking pissed because y'all fuck ass gave me the wrong GPS tag. When I kicked the fucking door in it was two old muthafuckin' crackas there watching fucking Jeopardy, I just knew I was in the wrong muthafuckin' place. I hurried up and got my ass up out of there before I caught a thousand years. I felt that y'all tried me for real and I wanted to kick both of your asses to sleep." barked Odell as he straightened Moe and Chi-Chi.

"I don't know! You're the only one who knew about us and where these niggas was at!" stated Moneisha.

"Cuz, are you fucking crazy or stupid? These niggas probably got a thousand niggas aiming at their heads, from homeboys to niggas they probably just do business with. Anybody could have ran up in them niggas shit." said Odell.

"You're right cuz!" interrupted Chineir "Because it's probably so many niggas who don't like them."

"Well, if you didn't do it, then who the fuck did it? It was three dead bodies in that house when the police took us out." said Moneisha.

"Hold up cuz, what the fuck you mean when the police took y'all out?"

"We went to jail, that shit was so crazy, and this detective dude was trying to frame us. He probably would've killed me!" said Chineir.

"What you mean he probably would've killed you?" asked Odell, ready to get crunk about his cousins.

"The detective, that's how my eye got like this. If it wasn't from the police officer that helped us escape out of their jail I don't know where in the hell I'd be. How do you think we made it home? That police guy..." Said Chineir.

"You mean to tell me that y'all escaped out of jail?"

"Hell yea cuz, because if we didn't they was going to lock us up forever." said Moe.

"Tell Odell everything." added Chineir.

"What you mean, everything?"

"Bitch, about the police car and how he talking about we owe him and shit!"

"Ohhhhh, yea cuz! Let me tell you how this muthafucka tried us. He got me and Chi-Chi's info, our numbers and all cuz. He even got yours too!" said Moneisha looking down at the floor, knowing damn well Odell was going to snap.

"Cuz, what the fuck you mean he got my number? HOW IN THE FUCK THE POLICE GOT MY NUMBER?"

"Because we gave it to him!" confessed Chineir.

"Why in the fuck did you do that, Twin?"

"Because we had no other choice, they were going to charge us with murder." said Moneisha.

"So y'all throw me under the bus! That's fucked up cuz and I didn't do a muthafuckin' thang." stressed Odell showing his frustration through his body language.

"It didn't go like that. We were put into the police car and me and Chi-Chi was talking about what happened because we thought it was you for real who came in there and killed them boys. But they were recording us and got the tape and promised he'll give it to us once he's finished with us!" said Moe.

"Oh yea! So he wanna play that game, huh? I got just the right thing for his crooked ass!" Odell addressed the twins as he tried to think of a devious plan to fuck this cop over for even thinking he was about to use his cousins. *And he had to be even super crazy to think I was going to do anything for his ass."* thought Odell.

"No Odell, let's do whatever this cop needs done, get the tape, and go on about our lives." said Chineir.

"Cuz, you know I don't fuck with no cops...PERIOD! So count me out because I ain't with it. All I have for him is a bullet in his head."

"But you have to help us. I know you're not going to let us go to prison for murder!" Said Chi-Chi trying to make her cousin Odell feel sorry for her.

"Cuz, I'm telling you right now, I'm only going to do this for you two muthafuckas because y'all my heart. But I promise you, the first time I feel this shit isn't on the up and up, I'm going to kill this cop."

"Alright cuz, but let's see what we have to do first and try to get this recording then you can do whatever you want to do." agreed Chineir.

"Okay, so when do we supposed to meet up with this crooked ass cop to see what the fuck he wants us to do?"

Asked Odell as he sat on the couch and bust down a sweet backwood, dumping the tobacco out into the ash tray that was sitting on the glass coffee table, filling it with high grade marijuana as he licked the outside, sealing the blunt. He lit it and took a deep pull, then another before he passed it to Chineir as she did the same thing and took a couple pulls, inhaling the toxins of the drugs before passing it to Moneisha. This was something they enjoyed doing each and every day. They called themselves the 'three amigos' when it came to smoking weed, especially the twins who felt they couldn't live without it.

"Y'all go ahead on and kill that blunt, I got a few runs to make. I'll get back up with y'all later. We ain't finished with this conversation! That shit you two did ain't cool at all, giving the fucking police my number. I'm going to have to go and grab me another phone later today because I'm not on that hot shit period. Y'all can keep in touch with that cop, I'm not doing it!" said Odell as he stood up with the bottom of his pants legs stuffed inside of the wheat colored Timberland boots.

Odell rarely wore shorts, especially throughout the day. But he had on a tank top with the massive Cuban link around his neck that hung to his stomach with an iced out medallion. He loved that flaussin shit. He always stayed jeweled up. He wore diamond rings on every finger, custom made earrings that was done in the design of a baking soda box. His teeth was all gold. He had his whole thirty-two teeth capped in rose gold and diamonds. Odell knew he was the shit. He had every bitch in the city on his dick. Every now and then he'd fuck around if a bitch caught him in that moment. But everybody knew he was locked in with this bad ass red, mixed looking bitch name Princess.

As Odell walked outside of the house, he put on a pair of Gucci shades as he hit the car alarm, disarming the Hawkeye alarm system he had installed on his Infiniti SUV. Hitting the remote start, the music instantly came on sounding like a concert. It was 8:15am and Odell didn't give a fuck about disturbing his neighbors. "FUCK'EM!" is how he felt. It was a lot of young bitches who stayed out there and this was how Odell let them know he was up and about. He noticed how hoes started walking outside, bringing the trash out while some checked their mailboxes like it was something in there, knowing damn well there wasn't anywhere in America where mail ran at eight in the morning. Once inside the SUV, Odell fired up the blunt he had in the ash tray from the day before that he never knocked off and pulled out of the yard. All the hot and sexy ass neighbors of his just looked in awe at the kandy colored outrageous orange Infinity SUV on thirty-two inch Forgiatos creep down the road and out of the gated community.

Chapter 19

King George had done made himself clear. He warned Tarrell that he hoped she wasn't nowhere involved in Devell's shooting. Tarrell wasn't trippin' about any of the threats because she knew that whatever investigation he had going on, that her name would come up clear. But what she didn't agree with was, the statement he made about taking Devell back to New York with him.

"Where in the fuck do he think I'm going when all of this happens?" thought Tarrell as she sat next to Ms. Barbara Jean on her left, trying to listen in on the conversation that Ms. Barbara Jean and Devell's friend was having. While Tarrell contemplated on whether or not she was going to put up a fight about her man leaving, because she didn't know what the fuck she'd do without him. Just when she was about to address the issue, the doctor came out.

"Excuse me, who is the closest to kin?" asked the doctor.

"That would be me." said Ms. Barbara Jean, "I'm his

mother. This is his fiancée" she said pointing at Tarrell. "And this is his brother. She also said as she continued. "Anything you have to say, you can say it in front of us all!"

"Well then, I would like to start by introducing myself. My name is Doctor Vernon Grant, M.D. I'm the top surgeon here at Winter Haven's Medical Center. I'm also the lead surgeon to your son's surgery and I can one hundred percent say that the surgery was a success."

The whole congregation that was still there couldn't help but hear the doctor as they eavesdropped on the doctor's words; the surgery was a success. Sending them into praise as they gave thanks to God. They put on a show, believing that it was their faith alone that saved Sister Barbara Jean's son. The doctor had a smile on his face, he loved his job and what he knew he was capable of doing. At first, he wasn't at all worried about this patient because it wasn't a part of his case load. To be honest, he was about to go home for the day. This patient belonged to Dr. Stanford. But when he was threatened, he had no other choice. Just looking at the menacing stare of this gangsta, he knew that those threats had truth in them so he did what he had to do and took charge of the surgery. Being that he was a senior doctor at Winter Haven's Medical Center, he had the power to do so.

Tarrell had to calm down Ms. Barbara Jean as she uncontrollably wept with joy. She thought she had lost her baby boy. There was nothing in the world that could prepare a mother for losing a child.

"So doc, can we see him?" asked King George.

"Yes, you all may. But could you do it one at a time, because he's in a critical state at the moment as he tries to recover from surgery. Any stress on him what-so-ever, we could lose him!" said Doctor Grant.

"I just want to see my boy!" cried out Ms. Barbara Jean.

"Okay, follow me ma'am. He's in recovery treatment on the third floor."

"Ma, you can go first when we get there, I'll go in after you then his peoples can go in after me." said King George demandingly.

Ms. Barbara Jean already knew who the menace was. She'd practically helped raise him along with her own son. She was more than glad to have him here because she knew her baby was safe with him around, and that he would get to the bottom of things if it was the last thing he did.

As the elevator made it to the third floor, the doctor led them all to the room they had Devell housed in and told them that if they needed anything to inform the nurse at the hallway desk. Ms. Barbara Jean paused for a moment and took a deep breath as she sent up a quick little prayer before entering the room.

"Lord please give me the strength and the ability to handle what I'm about to see. This is my son Lord, I shouldn't have to witness this, but I am at your mercy, for you know and does nothing but right. You giveth life and taketh away life. Let your will be done in Jesus name, Amen."

Once Ms. Barbara Jean made it inside she almost fell to her knees. Her baby boy was laying up on that bed with all types of tubes running in and out of his body. She heard the machines beeping with a steady beat every three seconds. That made her relax a little because she knew and felt that those beeps were a sign that her baby was alive somewhere up under there. At first Ms. Barbara Jean wasn't going to say anything, but how could she not. She had to let him hear her voice.

"Hey baby, what are you doing in here?" she playfully said. "You know I taught you how to be stronger than this, so if you can hear me, make your momma proud okay. I'm not going to disturb you much because you have some other people who's dying to get in here and see you. You always remember I love you son, and no matter what happens, I've always been proud of you!" said Ms. Barbara Jean as she leaned down and kissed her son on the forehead, leaving it soak and wet from the tears that fell out of her eyes. Ms. Barbara Jean was ready for King George to come in and talk to him. She knew that if he'd respond to anybody, that it would be him. When she made it outside the door she just nodded at him letting him know that it was his turn. Once he made it into the room, Ms. Barbara Jean lunged into Tarrell's arms and wept uncontrollably, unable to take seeing her son in the state that he was in.

"It's going to be okay momma. Everything is going to be okay. Watch my baby pull up out of this better than ever!" said Tarrell, trying to console her mother-in-law's pain as she stood there and let Ms. Barbara Jean get it all out.

King George couldn't believe what the fuck he was seeing. His main man and best friend was laid up in a hospital, shot up, damn near dead. Just the sight of Devell had King George's blood boiling. He couldn't even walk any closer. His legs had done froze up and his body was getting numb. This wasn't normal for him. He usually never visited a hospital or rarely gave a fuck about anybody. It was either you lived or you died fucking with him. So all this clinging to life shit wasn't cool as far as he saw it.

"I got you homie, you just get yourself together and I'm going to get you out of here, I promise you that. I found out a few people who was involved in this so I'm about to pay them a visit, you already know how I get down. It's an eye for an eye with me bro. Love ya nigga, and I'll holla back later." said King George as he spoke from a distance.

Feeling himself about to get all teary eyed, he exited the room and walked past Ms. Barbara Jean and Tarrell to the elevators as he made it outside to some fresh air.

"Ain't no way in hell a bitch gon' see me break down!" King George thought as he text Big-O on his phone and told him as soon as he's finish to hurry up and come get him.

****

Big-O had just made it to Pumpkin's house as he pulled the Humvee into the driveway. Big-O noticed this tall sexy ass bitch put a trash bag into the black two door Cadillac that was parked onto the driveway. As soon as she made it back inside the house, Big-O made his move and crept up to the front door, which was still wide open. Hearing her move about inside the house, Big-O slid in and closed the door behind himself, cutting out all the noise from the outside traffic that was passing by.

"Hello...Hello...Who is that?" asked Pumpkin as she made her way to the living room to see who the fuck it was that just closed her door. But when she saw Big-O she knew something was wrong. The look in his eyes told her that he didn't have any reasoning in his bones what-so-ever.

"What the fuck is you doing in my house? Skeeda ain't here!" she said, hoping this big ass nigga wasn't there to hurt her.

"Is your name Pumpkin?" asked Big-O.

"Yea, why?" she asked, afraid. "I can give you money, just don't hurt me." pleaded Pumpkin.

"Bitch, do it look like I came for any money?"

Right then Pumpkin knew she was in some deep shit.

Big-O saw the body of a man lying in the hallway and by the way this bitch was moving around, he knew the nigga had to be dead. Pumpkin tried to run, taking off full speed back towards the hallway, but she wasn't fast enough to get away from Big-O's swiftness as he caught her by the back of her hair that was hanging in a long pony tail style. He yanked her shit so fucking hard, he pulled the whole pony tail out from the root, making Pumpkin head look like she'd been scalped by an Indian.

"AAAAHHHHHHHHHHHHH!!" was all she could scream as her body followed the momentum of the snatch.

"Bring your bitch ass here!" ordered Big-O as he grabbed her around the neck and pulled her from behind into his embrace, wrapping his huge arms around her neck, choking the life out of her.

Pumpkin wasn't about to go out without a fight as she slung her arms wildly overhead, hitting her assailant upside his head, trying to get him to release his grip but none of it helped. All Pumpkin did was piss him off more. Big-O jerked her body up off the ground with a quick snatch and popped her neck, killing her in that instant as he slung her body across the arm ledge of the sofa, burying her face in its pillows. There wasn't a way in hell Big-O was going to leave and not see what the pussy was like. He took the bloody suit jacket off and undid his pants, pulling out his semi erect penis as he jacked it a few times getting it hard as a rock. Big-O wasn't working with much, he only had six inches of dick but he knew how to use it when it was time to throw down. Big-O slid up behind her and spreaded her legs apart and used his other hand to pull the loosely fit boy shorts to the side, revealing a pussy so fat. As soon as Big-O had the shorts pinned to one side, her pussy just popped out, looking like two full size bananas. Big-O took a finger and slid it through her shit wanting to taste her pussy. But when he brung his finger out, he couldn't possibly imagine tasting this bitch shit. Her pussy smelled rotten, and when he looked at his finger it was covered with an all-white film.

"This bitch gotta have some kind of infection!" thought Big-O not satisfied with just leaving because he was horny as hell. It's been quite a while and he needed him some pussy before he lost his mind. Big-O didn't have a condom on hand. He really didn't give a fuck about using them, but in this case he felt that if he fucked this bitch raw, he was

going to end up with something he couldn't get rid of.

Big-O still had his dick in his hand, slowly jacking it up and down as he continued to think what he was going to do and he fucked around and let the head of his dick rub across her pussy lips, sending chills through him that almost made him lose control. It was too late, before Big-O could think about anything else, he was all the way inside of her. He gripped her by the hips as he plunged in and out of her pussy uncontrollably. He was treating her like a rag doll, humping himself away at super-fast speeds. It wasn't even three minutes past and Big-O was nutting everywhere.

"OOOOOHHHH SHIT!!!" he screamed out loud as he tried to hump away, but it was no use. His body had become paralyzed as he stood froze inside of her. After a few seconds Big-O regained himself and marched down the hallway looking for a bathroom. "Damn this bitch was cold hearted!" thought Big-O as he stepped over the dead body that had an ax stuck inside of his skull.

Looking at the safe that stood there cut wide open, Big-O used his own intuition and thought... *"She must have come home and caught this nigga in her shit! That had to be what was inside of those trash bags she was putting inside the car. I have to get all of that."*

Big-O hurried up and cleaned himself off so he could get the fuck out of there. He noticed a can of lighter fluid on the bathroom shelf and grabbed it. *"Perfect"* he thought as he squirted some on the body in the hallway and on the bitch Pumpkin's body, using the rest on his jacket that had all of her blood on it. Big-O took the lighter out of his pants pocket and lit her ass up, doing the same to the body in the hallway. On the way back out, he kicked his jacket on the burning body as he witnessed it catch ablaze.

"Now, who's next?" said Big-O to himself as he looked inside of the two-door Cadillac CTS and saw just what it was he was looking for.

He grabbed the big ass trash bag and peeked inside. It was filled with money. He'd finally come up on a lick of his own. *"I can do me now, I'm tired of waiting on another nigga to eat before I can eat, or anything for that matter. Treating me like the help when we supposed to be friends."* Thought Big-O as he snatched up the bag and took it to the Humvee. Once inside, Big-O put a call in to King George who picked up on the second ring.

"Hello!?"

"That's taken care of!"

"Oh yea, that's what's up. How far are you away?" asked King George.

"A couple blocks, why, what's up?"

"Just get here, I'm about to fuck this city up. Ain't nobody getting away with hitting my nigga up." said King George as he ended the call.

"Should I tell him about the money or not?" thought Big-O as he turned into the hospital. *"Fuck that, I'm not telling this nigga shit. This my lick, all mines!"*

Chapter 20

When Big-O made it to the hospital, he didn't even have to park. King George was waiting outside, pacing back and forth until he spotted the Humvee coming towards him. Before the oversized SUV could come to a stop, he had the passenger door open and half way inside. By the time Big-O did stop, he knew something was wrong. He never witnessed his big homie act in such a way.

"Yo, what's up K.G.?" asked Big-O, hoping like hell he didn't know what just took place. How could he? He don't got no damn eyes on me like that! But for some reason, Big-O trembled with fear because he knew that his big homie King George seemed to know everything, and if he knew or found out about any of this, especially the money, then he had serious problems.

"What took you so long is what's up?!" said King George, already knowing what the fuck went down just by the sour ass smell that was lingering inside of the Humvee.

"It was more than one person there, but I took care of that shit with ease, boss." said Big-O trying to butter up the negative vibe he was receiving from his big homie.

"So, that shit official then?" said King George more of than asking as he continued. "Okay my nigga, but you gotta get this smell up out of here. I see you don't give a fuck who you stick your dick in!"

"I knew he knew! Damn, should I tell him about the money or what? Hell nawl, that's my come up. I'll deal with the consequences when they arrive." he thought before he spoke.

"So, where do you want to nap at?" referring to what hotel he wanted to stay at.

"It don't matter...well, yes it do! Take me to the Hampton Inn." said King George as he sat upright in the Humvee and played around with the search locater from the Humvee's media system. He was looking up the bitch Asia by her phone number that he had gotten from Damion's phone log.

"Bingo! This lil bitch bad." thought King George as he saw her picture pop up onto the screen. Going over her personal information, he saw where this bitch was born in 1998, making her only sixteen years old.

"This shit crazy for real, these niggas fucking these young ass hoes. All they asses need a bullet in their perverted head."

Mashing the save-to-file button on the touch screen, King George leaned back in the comfortness of the Humvee's passenger seat as he reminisced of all the good times and bad times him and Devell shared. "Somebody was in trouble, ain't no way a muthafucka was getting away from this." he thought as he dozed off, getting some much needed rest.

＊＊＊＊

Homicide Detective Gary Grant of the Polk County Sheriff's Office was furious. *"Ain't no way on this face of God's green earth that two suspects to a triple murder, both who were already in custody, just up and disappear and don't nobody know a fucking thing! I promise on my dead daddy's grave that whoever got something to do with this I'm gon' bury their ass as well as them two pretty bitches as soon as I run their asses down."* thought the detective as he looked over the surveillance footage with the surveillance officer, trying to see what the hell happened.

"Hold up! Roll that back!" asked Detective Grant as he focused on the pre-recorded video, hoping he didn't see what the fuck he thought he just saw. "Right there...now slow that down. Okay that's good. Now pause it. That son of a bitch, Officer Fulwiley!" barked the Detective as he hurried up and raced to his office and called the Captain, letting her know about the recent events and Officer Fulwiley's actions.

"Okay Detective, set up a briefing and I'll be there shortly. I hope you're right, because if not, Internal Affairs is going to be all over this." said Captain Cheryl Wertz, afraid to even touch this hunch from Detective Grant because she knew that he, as well as a few other officers in their division was under investigation for corrupt and rogue activities, and she didn't want shit to do with any of them.

"Captain, I have his ass on surveillance video helping

two murder suspects escape out of custody." said Detective Grant authoritatively, letting the captain know by the sound of his voice that he wasn't playing any games.

"I'll be there in thirty minutes, see you then Detective!" said Captain Wertz as she ended the call and rolled out of bed with her lover who was knocked out after all of their fucking, sucking, and role playing they'd just performed. She had never met a man who was able to stand up to her sexual appetite, let alone who was compatible and had so much in common with her. She was in love with Officer Fulwiley, and was willing to go the extra mile to save him from whatever danger that was awaiting. All she was able to do was pray and hope that he was clean. *"Please Lord, don't let me lose him. He's all I have!"* said Cheryl to herself as she sent up a prayer to God. Something that she hasn't done in over three years.

****

Old Man Larry and Joann had done made it back to Brandon Medical Center where Tenille and K-Boy was getting treated at. Larry recognized the group of police cars that was parked in the front as well as a few scattered about the front parking lot.

"Baby, you see what I see?" asked Larry, wanting to make sure he wasn't just trippin'.

"Yea, they got this place surrounded!" Joann replied and right that instant Larry knew he had to come up with a smooth plan to get Tenille and K-Boy out of there before the police apprehended them and took them into custody.

Scanning the area, Old Man Larry saw just what he needed, the ambulance garage. He parked the big white Ford Econoline off to the side, up under a sign that read 'EMPLOYEE'S ONLY'.

"Baby, we have to be quick, if they catch us then we're hit as well, and I'm too damn old for anybody jail cells." said Larry as he exited the van, followed by Joann as they walked up the wheelchair ramp, straight through the emergency shute. Coming up through the back entrance, they were only a few doors down from where they left Tenille and K-Boy. They slid into room #316 and thought of a plan, but it had to work. There wasn't room for error. When they'd finished devising their plan, Joann left and went to the second floor where she found an empty room and set it on fire. She didn't emerge until she saw it had caught ablaze and begin to spread. Rushing back to the elevator, it was just a matter of time before the fire alarm went off. As soon as Joann made it back into the room, Old Man Larry had two doctor jackets, which he gave Joann one to put on. He already had his on.

"Listen baby! As soon as the alarm goes off, we're going in. Our story is to evacuate these patients to the other side of the hospital for safety." instructed Larry.

"Okay baby!" eplied Joann as she buttoned up her jacket and slung the stethoscope around her neck on time as the fire alarm came to life, sounding out throughout the hospital. Larry looked out the door and saw everybody starting to race back and forth, even the officers that was on guard detail had done rushed off to see what the emergency was. That's when they learned about the fire that was rapidly spreading on the second floor. Remembering the oath they vowed to obey when they made it onto the police force, they instantly went to helping clear the area. That was just what Old Man Larry and Joann needed as they quickly made it to room #318, where Tenille and K-Boy looked at him and Joann.

"Old Man Larry! What the fuck are you doing here?" asked K-Boy, hoping Larry could tell him anything. Tenille just lit up with excitement. He knew somebody would soon show up, he was too important not to. But where was his family? Where was his bitches? All that ran through Tenille's head as it angered him, but little did he know, he was admitted under John Doe. That was the reason why nobody has shown up yet. Truth is, everybody that knew him was looking for him. The news about what happened was all over Bartow, and muthafuckas was ready to go to war for Tenille, not because they fucked with him like that, but because they represented Bartow, and Tenille was a product of Bartow.

"All of our asses is about to catch a million years once them crackers put one and two together about them dead bodies that was left in your trap." Said Old Man Larry as he caught both Tenille and K-Boy's attention when he mentioned dead bodies.

"Hurry up baby and get that bed detached!" Ordered Larry as he tried to move about in record time, before any cops showed back up. Joann was finished and ready. She had the bed with Tenille on it as she pushed it out and made her escape, going the opposite way of everybody else. Old

Man Larry and K-Boy was right behind them as they hooked the corner making their get-a-way as well.

"Hey, you, stop it right there!!" yelled the officer from way down the hallway.

"Hurry up baby!" said Joann as she held the ambulance entrance door open for Larry, helping him hide the bed on the other side of the doors wall. The police ran straight by, taking the loop shape hallway to the other side. Peeking through the bottom side of the window that was on the door, Old Man Larry saw it was clear and took off down the wheel chair ramp with K-Boy. Joann just followed suit. She was enjoying the excitement, it reminded her of back in the days.

As they made it to the van, Larry helped K-Boy inside and sat him in the second row seat, doing the same with Tenille, sitting him in the first row seat.

"Where the keys at baby?" asked Larry as he patted his pockets, knowing he had to have them because he was the one driving.

"They're in your left cargo pocket, baby!" said Joann, thinking; how in the hell could Larry function without her.

"Got'em, let's go sweetie!" he said, and they both hopped inside of the van and sped off.

"Baby, you know they're going to get us off the camera. What do you think?" said Joann, creating small talk, letting her man know that shit was about to get real ugly for them.

"I know baby girl, but I couldn't leave these two young soldiers in there and let them crackers railroad them. I'm too real for that baby!" replied Larry.

"So, where are we going?" she asked.

"To Tampa. We need a room so that we can figure out our next move, as well as make sure that them soldiers get the rest they need."

"Alright Daddy. I'm with you all the way. Even if it's straight to hell. I want to be the one kicking in the door!"

Larry knew Joann was gangsta, and there was no turning back. And he loved it when she called him Daddy, that shit turned Larry on. "Ain't no way in hell I'm gon' let my bitch meet the Devil first. I've waited way too long for that moment. She's going to have to follow me in!" thought Old Man Larry as he maneuvered the van in and out of traffic on highway 60 past Valrico and Riverview until he made it to Tampa city limits, turning right on highway 301 knowing exactly where he was headed, as he pulled into the LaQuinta Inn.

K-Boy didn't know what the fuck had happened, either the gunshot wound to the head, or the medical procedure at the hospital they performed on him took away any and all recollection of how in the hell he got to where he was at this very moment. And by looking at his cousin Tenille, it let him know whatever did happen, it had to be serious.

"Aye Larry!" said K-Boy.

"Yea, what's poppin' soldier?" replied Larry.

"Man, tell me what the fuck is going on? Please, just tell me something!" pleaded K-Boy.

"I got you. Just give me a moment soldier to get you two niggas in a room. I'll let you know everything I know."

Chapter 21

King George had done woke up from the deep sleep he was in. Thinking a lot of time had passed by, he checked his watch. Barely able to recognize the long hand from the short hand on the all bezzled out face on his Aqua Master, he took the back of his hand and wiped away the sleep from his eyes so he was able to clearly read the time.

"Five thirty!" Dammit, it's still early as fuck. I must have been sleep for only a few hours." said King George to himself, remembering it was only two-fifteen in the evening when they pulled up at the Hampton Inn. The king size, extra fluffy bed was too enticing to leave, but he knew he had to get up. He had business to take care of. Business that couldn't wait a moment longer.

King George grabbed his hygiene kit out of the carry-on bag he brought up with him and went inside of the oversized bathroom to wash his face and brush his mouth. *"Can't afford to be walking around with the stank mouth!"* He thought. After he finished up and got dressed, he put on a pair of black linen Gucci cargo pants, some all-black Gucci canvas chucks, and a black long sleeved button up Gucci silk shirt.

One thing King George specialized in was the order of fashion that he wore, he hated mix and match. Even if it was just some regular gym wear, it had to be Jordan everything, or Adidas everything; PERIOD.

"Let me get Big-O ass up, I bet his ass probably over there snoring up a storm!" he thought as he grabbed the key card to the room Big-O was staying in, which was the next room over. Both of them had keys to each other's room just in case of emergencies, and right now was an emergency. They were already behind schedule. He was tired and needed some rest but it was time to handle business and when it came to business King George didn't play around.

Sliding the key card in and opening the door, he saw Big-O sitting up on the bed, surrounded by bundles of cash. As he continued to count the money he had piled up in front of him, Big-O didn't even hear King George come in because of the T.V.'s loud volume. Big-O was watching the Fuse channel Top 100 Countdown of the year for best collaborations. "If it was one thing I knew, that was money! It had to be at least a couple million dollars laid across that bed." he thought as he cleared his throat purposely, gaining Big-O's attention.

"Damn big homie, what you sneaking up on a nigga for?" said Big-O in a joking manner, trying to act as if he wasn't doing shit wrong.

"What's up with you?" asked King George, because

something had to have happened and he needed to know. This was just way too much money. Somebody had to have lost their life over this, and ain't no way in hell he was about to be in the blind!" He thought.

"What do you mean ,what's up?'" replied Big-O, still not looking up, afraid to lock eyes with his big homie.

"Nigga, this muthafucking money you're counting up. Where the fuck that shit come from?"

"Oh! I got this from that hit earlier on that bitch Pumpkin. She was about to get ghost, but I ran down on that ass before she could make it out the door."

"So, why you ain't fill me in on any of this, what we cuffing now?" asked King George menacingly.

"Nawl K.G.! It ain't nothing like that. I just wanted to count it before I broke you off half." said Big-O lying through his teeth. He had no intentions on giving King George shit.

"My nigga, you on some fuck ass, hoe nigga shit, and I don't wanna be fucked up with you period!"

"What you mean big homie? This shit ain't that serious. You think I'm on some hoe shit? You can have all of this shit...here, take it!" begged Big-O not knowing his greediness had just turned his friendship with his childhood friend sour.

"Nawl, I'm good. You enjoy that shit, but lose my number for good. I should've let Devell kill your ass years ago when you broke inside his crib and stole those two bricks, but no, I covered that shit and tried to show you what being real was, but I see you don't have a real bone in your body." said King George as he continued on. "You just like any other nigga to me now!" and before Big-O could say anything else, he was out of the room, heading back to his room next door.

Just thinking about the little episode that just transpired between them two had him furious. Not because of the money, but because he had this unloyal ass nigga around him day in and day out. *"I should put a bullet in this nigga head!"* he thought as he grabbed his bags and left the room with no intentions on ever coming back. *"Fuck the eight days the room was paid for."*

As he made it to the Humvee, he opened the back cab and grabbed the titanium case out, replacing it with his luggage. He put the case on the passenger seat in the front, punched in the security code, opening it up as he checked its contents to make sure that everything was still intact, which it was. There was four high powered explosive devices, each with its very own detonator switch. Smiling to himself, he was ready for some fun. he could already taste the blood as he made his way into traffic, heading to his next destination; Saint Paul Project's. "Where you at Asia?" He mumbled to himself as he thought of fucking the lil young bitch before he took her life away.

****

Odell hit the block in his Infinity SUV. Lincoln Avenue was on swole today, muthafuckas was out of school and every bitch in the hood was hanging out. The weed had him feeling extra good and he had his eyes already glued on this lil young bad bitch he knew that went to the high school. Her name was Pharah. She was nineteen years old and the bitch was bad. A black Barbie looking muthafucka. The Outrageous kandy paint had Odell's Infinity looking like a pack of Jolly Ranchers how it kept changing color after color right before your eyes.

Odell was playing that new Boosie song 'Face Down' as he pulled up and stopped right in front of the bus stop bench. It was covered with hoes like they were a swarm of bees. Bitches was sitting on the bench, on the back of the bench, on each other's lap, and some was just standing around. They called themselves the 'Dope Girl Divas' because all they fucked with was dope boys, and Odell was one of the biggest niggas in the dope game they knew, and he was around their age. Well, not really. But he wasn't much older than them. You should've seen how them hoes went crazy when Odell opened up all of his doors, lifting the front ones up in the air as he crunk up his music all the way. He hid his eyes behind the Gucci shades he was wearing as he watched them hoes come alive, surrounding his shit dancing, busting the latest moves. When the last verse came on, which was Boosie's verse, they went extra crazy, throwing their hands up and singing along;

"I got a fire red bone who go all night long-BOOSIE
She like her ass tooted up and her face down
She like her ass tooted up and her face down
She like her ass tooted up and her face down
Face down...Face down
She like her ass tooted up and her face down
Face down...Face down
She like her ass totted up and her face down

I got a chick out Mississippi, she cold too
Thick thighs, nice legs, soul food."

Odell knew how to get them lil young hoes started. Whatever his plan was had worked. The bitch Pharah was locked in and staring his ass down as if she wanted to fuck him right there in the middle of the road. Odell was closing his doors as he walked around his SUV. He knew that this was the moment to bust his move, if he ever had one. He nodded his head, indicating for her to come here. Usually Pharah would play hard to get, but she wasn't about to miss this opportunity and let him pass her up and choose one of her friends, because them hoes wouldn't hesitate to get at his sexy ass.

Pharah walked up to Odell and leaned in, pressing her perky 35 cup size breast against his body. Odell didn't even hesitate as he pitched his game at her.

"So, is you a lil girl who's scared to fuck, or, is you 'bout your business and is going to let me tap that ass? Because I don't got time to be wasting."

"Shit, I'm 'bout whatever as long as you treating, and since you ain't looking for a young girl, just make sure you tip me like a grown woman!" she said, knowing she wasn't fucking or sucking this nigga dick for free. he had to at least drop a hundred on her, she ain't just started this shit.

"Get your ass in!" demanded Odell as he got in and rolled all the windows up. Pharah waved at her friends goodbye as she jumped in the passenger side and wiggled on the Ostrich seats, making herself comfortable.

"You smoke?" asked Odell.

"Hell yea, you got some?"

"Yea, but you have to roll up. You think you can handle that?"

"Nigga please, I'm a beast. Where that shit at?" she said with confidence as she held her hand out.

Odell reached in the middle console where he kept his personal stash of high grade marijuana at and grabbed two fat ass buds out of the bag. Pharah knew a lil something about weed, the basics. She knew what Reggie was, and Zona. None of those looked like the shit she had in her hand. This weed was a lime green, with reddish orange spots all over it, sprinkled with little white dots like it was covered in snow.

Pharah couldn't wait to fill her lungs up with it. Just the thought of the weed had her horny as hell, she was able to feel the juices in her pussy begin to flow. Odell handed her the sweet flavored Backwood blunt as he waited for a second to see lil momma do her thang. Odell was surprised at how she ripped the blunt apart and layered it piece by piece, building a lil canoe. She took the two buds and crumbled them into the blunt, pressing all of its contents inside so it didn't waste over onto the seats. Pharah knew some niggas tripped about something so petty, and she didn't want this nigga to act up on her. She was actually really feeling dude for some reason.

Once Pharah got the blunt packed how she wanted it, she noticed Odell looking at her as she did her thang. She was just about to lick it seal, but instead, she took her hand and reached down between her legs, moving her three inch boy shorts to the side. She rubbed her two fingers through her pussy lips soaking the shit out of them as she took the juices from her pussy and rubbed it across the tightly twisted blunt, sealing it for good. Even though she didn't have to do it again because she knew her shit, Pharah still repeated the process, soaking the blunt with her sweet tasting pussy juices, licking her fingers dry, passing the blunt under her nose, enjoying the smell.

"You ready to smoke some pussy?" Asked Pharah as she released a seductive smirk on her face as she thought about the nasty and freaky shit she was about to do to this nigga.

"Here!" Said Odell, throwing her the lighter, wanting to see this bitch smoke her own pussy first. But for some reason, he was anticipating smoking this blunt, just the thought of it being soaked in pussy juice had Odell's dick rock hard. *"Fuck! I want to taste that pussy for real!"* was running through his mind as he imagined eating her pussy from the front, the back, the sides, even upside down while the bitch did a hand stand. Odell was a freak, and a violent one at that. He felt that he wanted his way in the bedroom, and if he didn't get it, then he would forcefully have his way.

Pharah had done fired the blunt up and took a hard and long pull, pausing for about ten seconds before blowing a cloud of smoke out of her nose like a raging bull in the winter time. She took another pull, then another before she passed the blunt to Odell. The marijuana was so potent it had her experiencing multiple effects at the same time. She wanted to relax but her sex drive was rapidly building up. Usually she could control it but right now her sexual libido took over her mind. Odell was trying to savor the taste of the fire ass weed soaked with this bad bitch pussy juice as he leaned back in the driver's seat and pulled on the blunt repetitively, blowing the smoke out his mouth inhaling it back through his nose giving himself his own shot gun rush. He felt something jerk at his pants around the waist line, demanding his attention. Odell looked down from behind the Gucci shades where he caught the freak bitch he had in his passenger seat unbuttoning his True Religion jeans, pulling his dick out through the middle of his boxer briefs.

"Oooohhh wheh! That's a big ass dick!" said Pharah as she turned facing Odell in a Chinese style position as she leaned in and licked the side of his dick from the base all the way to the head.

"I ain't never sucked a dick this big before!"

"So what, you're scared? If you're scared, you can go on about your business because I don't have time to be playing lil girl games with you." said Odell, trying to amp her ass up because he knew this lil bitch had to know how to suck a dick. Her mouth and lips was designed for dick sucking. She had those pointy, poked out, fish looking lips, looking all exciting, like a nasty ass porn star.

Pharah wasn't nobody's lil girl, and she was about to show this nigga how serious her head game was as she gripped it at the bottom and pointed it at her mouth as she stretched her lips and jaws as wide as she could until over half of Odell's nine inches was banging on the back of her throat. She closed her mouth down and twirled her tongue around his dick head as it sliced through the middle of his pee hole, sending a tingling sensation through his whole body.

"GOD DAMN BITCH! NOW THAT'S WHAT I'M TALKING 'BOUT!" said Odell as he ran his right-hand fingers over the nape of her neck. Pharah knew what that was a sign of, she had done fucked him up already and she wasn't even in her groove yet. Pharah's mouth got just as wet as her pussy whenever she sucked a dick. She started to jack on it slowly as she worked the head of his dick, sucking and popping it with her lips; A little trick that she specialized in. She had done got in rhythm as she started to work the back side of his dick, licking it right by the nut sack, rubbing the head of his dick with the palm of her hand, causing an electric like friction, sending Odell's mind into overdrive. Never has he ever had a bitch suck his dick like this animal ass bitch was sucking him up right now. Pharah felt the tension building up as Odell's dick started to swell up and throb in her hand. That's when she went for the kill. She put his dick back in her mouth and slowly sucked and slurped it up and down. She looked up at him and his Gucci shades had done disappeared. She noticed his eyes was rolled all the way in the back of his head. Pharah had done stretched both of her hands across Odell as she braced herself on the driver's door, sucking that dick with no hands, just using straight jaw muscles. He was about to cum because she was pulling the pre-cum up out of him as she sucked his dick like a professional.

"That's it, that's it. Oooh shit, that's it right there...Suck this dick bitch. Suck it. Suck it. Oooooooohhh sssssshhhhhhiiiit!" Odell screamed out like a wild untamed animal unable to hold it any longer. He released everything he had inside of him into her mouth.

Pharah turned it up a notch. She went to jerking the while she sucked the head.

"Get it all out. You better not stop nigga. Nut in my mouth!" mumbled Pharah as she came up for a second and swallowed all the nut she had in her mouth as she continued jacking and jerking on his dick, catching the rest of his nut on her face as she wrapped her lips back around his dick and sucked on it until it disappeared in her mouth.

When Pharah came up, she noticed they was still parked on the side of the curb. They haven't moved an inch. She noticed all her hoes was watching through this nigga's window in amazement. They all knew Pharah was a beast. She was a force to reckon with when it came to sucking dick, fucking, or just playing niggas. They were no comparison. When they all started to clap, it gained Odell's attention. He was in disbelief as he saw his truck surrounded by nothing but bad bitches as they clapped and cheered their home girl on, giving her a standing ovation. Never in his life has Odell ever imagined being in the center of such attention.

He put his dick back in his briefs and buttoned his jeans back up, cutting the music down before he spoke.

"I gotta give it to you, you're a fucking beast and I'll fuck with you anytime anywhere. I see we gave your lil friends a peep show, huh?" said Odell as he waited on a response but all he got was a seductive stare down. Pharah knew better than to overdo it and act like she was a groupie. She was a bad bitch and she knew it. She was going to wait on him to take it further, and if he didn't, then so be it. *'I'll see you soon!'* she thought.

"So, when do you want to hook up again?" he asked.

"It don't matter to me. You know, school is out so I just be hanging with my girls here!"

"You got a phone number, or some way I can reach you?" asked Odell.

"Yea, I got a phone, but it's off right now. I'm going to pay the bill Friday when my momma give me my allowance."

"ALLOWANCE! You mean to tell me, muthafuckas still get allowances?"

"I can't speak for everybody else, only for myself and my momma spoils me. You can't tell? What, I don't look like I supposed to be spoiled?" asked Pharah knowing damn well she looked the part and then some.

"Allowance ain't the word for it, a nigga will have your ass stuntin' like a real boss bitch!"

"Yea right, don't be trying to blow my head up because I'm not no lil lame ass girl!"

"If I thought you was one of them, you wouldn't be sitting on that Ostrich right now. I don't fuck with lames!" barked Odell.

"Okay then, I can stand to be straightened, so what we gon' do? I mean, how do we connect again? Or, is you just planning on sliding through whenever you need me to suck your dick?" asked Pharah, because she was feeling Odell and wanted to fuck with him a lot more. Maybe see if he meant it when he said he'll have me stuntin' like a boss bitch. Odell pulled out his touch screen phone and went straight to his phone book and selected; add new contact.

"What's your number?"

"You might as well give me yours. I told you my phone was off until Friday, I can call you from one of my friend's phone."

"Nahl, we ain't gon' do none of that. I don't play people having my number like that!" said Odell as he reached into his jeans pocket and pulled out a fat ass bank roll. All Pharah saw was hundreds as she watched him flip through the bills, tearing off a pile of the big face hundreds, handing them to her.

"What's this for?" she asked.

"That's for you. Get that phone turned back on so I can call you for starters! Now, what was that number?" Odell asked with an arrogant smirk on his face. Pharah didn't hesitate as she read off the digits.

"It's 289-1666! And you better call me!"

"Oh, you ain't gotta worry about that. You just better answer or else!"

"What you mean, or else?"

"Act like you don't know what the fuck I mean."

"I hope you ain't the violent type. I'm not with that domestic shit. If you on that, then you can get your money back!" said Pharah seriously.

"Nah baby girl, we good. I'm just fucking with you." said Odell, knowing damn well he was dead ass serious. Ain't no way in hell he was going to let another nigga get that fire ass head she got. "I'll beat this bitch to death." he thought as he locked her number in under private.

"Can I get a hug before I leave?" asked Pharah.

"Yea, come here!"

Pharah leaned in and wrapped her arms around his neck and gave him a real tight hug as she kissed him before she released her embrace, allowing her tongue to roam the inside of his mouth. She pulled back. She knew she had him. Just thinking about the stack he had just dropped on her had Pharah ready to go to the drawing board to prepare for round two.

She opened the door and stepped out of his Infiniti SUV, arching her back as her high heels landed on the side bar, using the extra help as she made it to the ground. Feeling her boy shorts all in her ass cheeks, Pharah didn't even think about pulling her shorts down. She let her cheeks hang all the way out as she walked out about ten feet in front of his whip so he had a clear view of her and that's when she gave it to him and put on one of stankest walks she could perform. Pharah was super bad. She stood five foot eight, weighing 160 pounds. She was slightly bow-legged with some thick ass thighs, small waist line and big ass booty. Her shit was real though, and it jiggled like jelly when she walked, hypnotizing most niggas that got caught in its wrath. She had the perfect size breast. They stood at attention without a bra. Her measurements were 35-26-42. Pharah had real grey eyes and wore her hair in a short wrap cut that curled in up under her ears, giving her face a professional look while her body took muthafuckas breath away.

"Un Un Bitch! Walk it out hoe!" said Erica Lewis, Pharah's best friend as she clapped her partner in crime on.

"Aie, Aie, Aie, Aie!" they all chanted as they

surrounded Pharah and went to twerking to the sounds of Odell's music as he turned up his stereo system before he pulled off.

Erica pulled Pharah up to her close like they was dyking so she could whisper in her ear.

"Bitch, I recorded everything!"

"Hoe, stop lying!" replied Pharah shocked.

"Bitch, I got it all. I'm talking about everything. You had that nigga eyes in the back of his head."

"Hoe, let me see it, you know I gotta make sure I did my thang."

"Oh, trust me bitch, you killed it."

All that Pharah could think of was black mailing this nigga. She had her mill ticket and was most definitely going to cash in on it.

"Either he pay me or I sell it to his bitch! Everybody know his bitch Princess is the plug." she thought as she waved him goodbye as the pretty truck turned away.

Chapter 22

It was getting darker by the seconds as King George made it out to Spirit Lake Road, coming up from Wrecker Highway.

"I wonder if the alley is still behind the bank!" he thought as he pulled into the parking lot and whipped the Humvee around back, blending the massive black SUV in with the darkness. Putting the high beams on, he saw that it was a lot of bushes, damn near looked like a forest area but he was still able to see the open pathway that separated Saint Paul Project's from the bank's parking lot. The path was about thirty feet, a big ass sand dune. King George put the Humvee in four-wheel drive as he attacked the trail. He remembered back in the days when they use to come through here, this very same path. Except back then, it wasn't no bushes surrounding it and the path had a big ass dirt hill at the beginning, like a ramp, and niggas from everywhere use to come out to Saint Paul on dirt bikes, four wheelers, three wheelers, and any other kind of machine that they thought they could jump the dirt ramp with. King

George had a two stroke Banshee that had extra modifications done, he used to call out everybody. Any nigga that thought they shit was faster, all you had to do was put up the ten stacks and line that shit up.

The drive through Saint Paul was about a quarter mile long, straight away stretch. And to end the race, you had to jump the ramp. *"I use to kill that shit!"* thought King George as he took him a ride back down memory lane, reminiscing about the niggas he grew up with.

"I gotta check up on them fools before I leave." he mumbled to himself as the military style vehicle crept through the thick sand like it was pavement. The Humvee was designed to conquer rough terrain. Making it through to the other side, he cut off the lights and parked behind the last block of project buildings that sat off to the right. Checking the profile chart on the Global Positioning screen, he had to make sure he had the right address, couldn't afford to bring that unwanted heat blowing up the wrong apartment.

"Building 'H', apartment #327" read the address up under Asia's school I.D. profile. "Bitch, I hope you done said your prayers and found peace with God!" thought King George as he took one of the explosive devices out of the titanium case, as well as its detonator and placed it inside his left cargo pants pocket. He also grabbed the special designed Glock.50 that he had modified with a military grade silencer, placing it into the shoulder strap he had just put on. This is what he hated so much about Polk County, and why he moved away in the first place, shit was just too wide open. A muthafucka could spot you from a mile away, and in the line of work he was in, King George knew he needed the big city to camouflage and hide his entire existence. But right now, he had to bend a set of rules he declared he would forever live by, and that was to never commit another crime in Winter Haven, Florida. Especially after it took over nine years to overturn a thirty-year sentence from fleeing from the police, afraid to violate his probation. His main man and best friend was laying up in a hospital near death. If he had to burn this whole city down and risk losing his own life, then so be it, but they were about to feel his wrath one way or the other.

Leaving the SUV on as he exited, he looked around for the correct housing building. It was so many buildings out there and with the street lights out it was hard to notice any building numbers or letters without walking up on each and every building. Regardless of what it was that he had to do, he had to get it done. He crept alongside one of the buildings that sat right in front of where he had the Humvee parked and walked around the side to get a clear look at the front to see which building he was at.

To his luck, the building he was standing in front of was 'H', the same identical building that was on Asia's information. "Apartment #327, #327, #327, where are you?" spoke King George to himself as he read the number on the first apartment door, following them all the way down. "#321, #323, #325..., here we go, #327. Hearing the noise in the background, King George knew somebody had to be home. He gently turned the doorknob to see if it was locked or not, and to his luck it was unlocked. He pulled his Glock.50 out and positioned himself as he entered the apartment. He realized the noise he was hearing must've came from the T.V. set that was on, blaring loudly. He quickly scanned the area and saw there was nobody in sight, just a small plasma mounted on the wall, playing re-runs of Martin.

"So far so good!" he thought, knowing the T.V.'s volume was perfect, just in case he made any noise, it would be blended in with the noise that was already blaring out of the tiny surround sound speakers it was attached to. As he made it to the hallway of the apartment, he noticed someone was there as the shadow from the bathroom illuminated through the hallway's darkness. Peeping through the cracked door of the bathroom, he was able to see her as she looked in the mirror at her nakedness. As she lotioned her body down with the Avocado scented lotion by Blithe & Bonny, King George just stood there, blended in with the hallway, staring at the exotic creature. *"This can't be her!"* he thought to himself as he lustfully stared at Asia, who had to have looked every bit of twenty-five, with a body most porn stars would kill for. This bitch was only sixteen with a 36-24-48 body, standing at six foot two, 194 pounds. This bitch was bad to death and King George had to have him some of her.

"What the fuck is they feeding these young muthafuckas now-a-days?" he thought as he slid on by the cracked bathroom door, deep into the apartment to make sure that nobody was home. The apartment was only a two bedroom, one bath. What more would you expect living in the project's. Checking the room on the right, he saw it was empty and looked like it belonged to an older woman with

how she had Avon products lined all up across the dresser.

"This must be the bitch momma's room. If the bitch bad like her daughter, I might just wait a few and have me a two for one treat!" thought King George as he leaped back across the darkened hallway to the room directly across from it, maneuvering like he was in the military on some espionage shit. The door to this room was locked. King George grabbed the door handle and tried opening it. The knob turned but the door didn't budge. This shit was crazy because he had to get into this room, ain't no way he was going to leave any stones unturned. Trying not to make any noise, he leaned in on the door using his right shoulder to try and bust through as quietly as he could, but it was no help. As soon as he pushed it out of its death grip, it had the loudest squeak you ever heard. *"FUCK!!"* screamed King George silently as he hurried inside the room and posted up against the wall out of sight.

"Hello! Who is that? That's you momma? What are you doing in my room?" asked Asia from afar, knowing damn well she had to be in there trying to snoop around for money so she can buy drugs to quench her crack habit. "I'm telling you momma, I'm not playing with your ass this time. If you're in my shit, I'm going to beat your muthafucking ass!" Yelled Asia as she bounced out of the bathroom butt ass naked to see who in the fuck was in her room. Just hearing this young reckless bitch run foul at the mouth thinking he was her mother had King George furious, ready to put a bullet straight through this bitch brain.

It was show time for him, fuck hiding on this bitch. Now she'll get to witness first-hand what it means to shorten your days by disrespecting your parents. Asia came storming into the room with her fist balled up ready to knock the lights out of her mother, but instead she came face to face with the barrel of the silencer as it stuck an extra six inches from the original barrel of her intruder's gun.

"AHHHHHHHH!" she screamed as she threw her hands and arms up in a defensive mode, scared to death of the intruder that was inside of their apartment, in her room.

"Bitch, shut the fuck up and stand your bitch ass straight up before I put a bullet in your fuck ass!" ordered King George as he ran his finger across the wall and flipped on the light switch. He thought what he saw when he peeped through her bathroom was bad. That was an understatement. This bitch was standing at eye level with him, and she was bad. She had a baby doll face with natural dimples. Her skin complexion was high yellow and her full breast didn't have one bit of sag to them as they stood out at attention towards him, displaying their firmness. Her stomach looked as if she did sit ups and crunches on a regular. She had a ring attached to her naval, bringing more sex appeal to what looked like the perfect, sexiest woman he'd ever laid eyes on. Her waist was flawless and right beneath her hips spreaded as King George followed her posture all the way to the floor at her perfectly manicured toes.

"Bitch you bad!" confessed King George as he gave her props. At that moment, he wanted to tie her ass up and fly her back to New York with him.

Asia knew she had to bust a move quick. She'd never been in a situation like this where she was the victim. She done been on missions with Damion before and saw all the treacherous shit he's done to niggas. He even let her put work in on a nigga before when she shot one of his workers for coming up short on his money. She scanned this nigga who stood directly in front of her up and down noticing the way he was dressed. Ain't no way in hell this nigga had what her nigga had in him. For a second there, she acted as if she wanted to reach for the gun. *"I could take that gun from his bitch ass!"* she thought, until she was able to stare into his eyes and she knew right then that whoever this man was that had her at gun point was pure evil.

A small tear rolled down her left cheek and all she thought about then was; if she was going to make it out of this alive. "Where was Damion Grey when she needed him?"

"Bitch, you got one of two choices if you want to live!" he barked at her.

She thought she'd talk a little shit just to stall for time, hoping that somebody would show up. Hell, anybody would do right now.

"Do you know who the fuck my man is?" barked back Asia, hoping that he'll ask who and when she say Damion's name, he'll take off runnin, begging for his own life. But little did she know, Damion Grey's resume wasn't a fraction of the killer's that was standing in front of her.

"Nah, I don't know who your nigga is. What, am I supposed to know him or something?"

She had the floor and she took advantage of it. Now it

was her turn to bring fear to his ass. "My man is Damion!" She said pausing as she put a smile on her face, waiting for some sort of fearful sign. But instead, she got the shit slapped out of her as King George came up with his back hand and damn near knocked her ass out.

"Bitch, what! I supposed to be scared or something? What the fuck do you think I'm here for? I'm not running from him, I'm hunting him and I won't stop until everybody he loves or fuck with is dead."

The backhand blow had Asia's head spinning, she had developed a migraine instantly.

"What the fuck was that for?" she screamed at him, but King George not knowing this was right up her alley. She loved to get abused, especially before sex and now she was wondering if this mystery man could fuck as hard as he could hit.

It was the name that she mentioned that drove him furious. Here this nigga done shot up his best friend and she wanted him to fear his name. "She lucky it ain't a bullet in her head already!" He thought.

"Listen carefully because I'm going to only tell you this once. So if you want to live, then you'll do everything that I tell you to do...do I make myself clear?"

Asia was willing and ready to do anything to save her own life, she wasn't even seventeen yet. Ain't no way in hell she was ready to die.

"Okay, what do you want from me?" she asked, trying to act like a scared victim, covering her breast with her arms.

"Get your fuck ass over there!" ordered King George

as he used the gun and pointed it at the bed, guiding her all the way as she sat on the edge of the single size bed that looked two sizes too small for this big ass bitch.

"Nah, don't sit your ass down, bitch get on all fours!"

"What you mean, all fours?" she asked.

"Bitch, you ever got fucked from the back?" asked King George as he shook his head from left to right in disbelief at this slow ass bitch. *"She's the true definition of all beauty and no brains."* he thought as he walked up behind her and ran his index and bird finger of his left hand all up through her pussy.

Asia's pussy was so wet, she imagined the way this nigga would fuck her.

"I wonder if he has a big dick?" was just one of the few things that had her mind racing. As soon as King George pulled his hand out of her pussy and back out through her ass cheeks, she had done hypnotized him how she did one of her little tricks making both of her ass cheeks dance as she looked back at him all seductively with her thin tongue stretched out licking across her own lips.

King George damn near tore the front of his linen pants as he just snatched them down far enough to pull out his dick. Asia tried to get a good look at what he was working with but fucked around and moved a bit too fast, making her catch a quick knot upside the head as King George tapped her upside the head with the barrel of his gun.

"OUUCCHH!!, what the fuck was that for?" asked Asia as she grabbed the spot she got hit at, trying to massage it, but it was too late because she felt the instant knot.

"Bitch, I ain't tell you to move. Now next time you try that shit, I'mma put a bullet in your ass."

"Damn nigga, I was just trying to see what the dick look like before you fuck me. I see you like to beat on bitches, huh?"

"Yea, especially hoes that can't follow orders." said King George speaking to deaf ears because all Asia could think about was the glimpse of his dick she just saw.

Her mouth was watering up, she wanted it in her mouth so bad, but right now she knew that was out of the question. But for now she just needed to make it through this alive. She knew how good her pussy was and knew without a doubt that he'd be back.

Getting the situation under control, King George eased all the way up to the end of the bed and grabbed Asia by the waist, pulling her, making her crawl back on her knees and hands like a panther sensing danger. Taking his dick, he rubbed it through her cheeks, allowing the dick head to slide across her pussy.

"OOHHH Shit!!!" moaned Asia. She wanted it inside of her right now. She was a cold blooded freak and was feeling like a crack head do when they don't have any drugs.

His dick was as hard as a rock right now, it was standing straight out at attention, all ten inches of it. He placed the gun back inside of the shoulder holster he had on and used both hands to spread her cheeks open. Just the softness of this bitch skin made him fall in love with her ass for the moment.

"Shittt!!" mumbled King George to himself as he saw her whole backside open up. Her asshole was open, her pussy was open and had a streak of curly hair running through her like she was Dominican or something. He couldn't help himself, he had to taste the pussy as he leaned down and ran his tongue across her clit all the way back up to her ass hole.

"GOTTT DAMMMMN NIGGGGA! What the fuck is you trying to do to me?" said Asia, burying her whole face in the pillow. Just that one lick almost made her bust a nut. With his hands on her cheeks, he kept her wide open as he directed his dick inside her pussy with no hands. This young bitch pussy felt so good, it was so tight and so warm. He pictured fucking this bitch forever. He tried to take his time and slide all of his ten inches in her just to get her pussy loose and let her feel what all she had to get adjusted to. But Asia wasn't having it. She backed up so hard on his dick, she felt it as it touched the base of her stomach.

"Oh yesss! Now fuck me!" she moaned, knowing she done finally found a dick that would satisfy her.

"One thing she didn't have to worry about and that was getting the shit fucked out of her." Thought King George as he found himself a rhythm and started to long stroke her, watching his dick as it slid in and out of her fat pink pussy. Her pussy was so wet, it looked like she was leaking on him, pussy juice was dripping off his dick every time he came out of her.

"You like that tight wet pussy don't you? Go ahead, you can tell me. It's only you and me here!" said Asia, she loved to talk dirty during sex, but she see she wasn't getting any feedback as her mystery man just kept long dicking her ass to death. Usually she would have to get a nigga to finger her ass to get her to climax, but not now, this nigga was hitting every one of her g-spots imaginable. She still used her ass muscles, making her shit hole open and close. King George couldn't believe what he was seeing this young red bitch do. This bitch was taking all of him like she was a grown woman, and he was loving it too. He kept trying to block out the conversation she was making, he hated to talk or say anything until he was ready to nut but for some strange reason, he was liking everything she was saying.

"Got damn nigga, put all of it inside of me! Fuck me harder, fuck me harder, fuck me harder...please!" was all you heard besides their bodies and noise it made as he collided with her cheeks over and over, "Splat, Splat, Splat, Splat, Splat." He knew she was about to cum how her pussy tensed up and started to automatically grip his dick as her rhythm stopped. She went from throwing it back to damn near zombie mode, but none of that stopped King George, he was about to cum as well. His speed was uncontrollable as he pumped away, hitting every wall and corner that she possessed inside her pussy.

"I'm cummin, got damn I'm cummin! You better not stop! Fuck me, please fuck me." she screamed out, but she wasn't by herself. They both was about to cum at the same time.

"Damn shawty, this pussy soo..." and before he could say good, he had done pulled out and skeeted all over her ass cheeks.

"Nooo, what are you doing? Put it back in, please!" begged Asia wanting him to nut inside of her, just in case what Damion had dumped in her wasn't any good, she was determined to have her a baby.

King George grabbed some pink lace panties that was lying on the dresser and wiped his dick off. It really was no use trying to wipe off because his whole mid-section was soaked. But it was worth it, he needed a good fuck. Now it was back to business. Seeing him grab his gun out of his shoulder holster, Asia thought he reneged on his proposition.

"What are you doing? You said if I did as you say you would spare me my life!" she pleaded.

"You're right. I'm just preparing myself. You're lucky because I came to kill you, so don't make me change my mind!"

"Will I ever see you again?" Asia asked as she thought about never having that big dick again.

"I don't know. Maybe!"

Walking back the same way he came, King George tried to adjust his vision back to the darkness of the hallway. Reaching into his side cargo pocket, he grabbed the explosive device and placed it inside the couch that sat by the door on his way out. Asia was still in her room, plundering for something to put on. She put on some grandma draws and a thin light blue Baby Phat sweat suit. Some no-show socks, and a pair of Carolina blue Jordan's. Grabbing her cell phone, she rushed behind him, but he was already gone. The door was still open to the apartment as Asia ran straight through it, looking left, then right. It was like he just disappeared out of thin air. She got scared all over again and began to scream at the top of her lungs, causing her neighbor from across the sidewalk to come out.

"Asia what's wrong? You better not be fighting your momma again!" said Ms. Kat, who's been living out there from what seemed like the beginning of time.

Sniffling between her sobs, she told Ms. Kat what just happened..."I got raped!"

"Who did this to you baby?" asked Ms. Kat, already on her cordless phone dialing 911.

"I don't know, I'm scared he's going to come back looking for me to kill me." confessed Asia.

"Come inside baby, and lock the door behind yourself while I go and get my gun." said Ms. Kat as she raced to her bedroom closet to retrieve her .38 special.

Unfortunately Asia wasn't able to lock the door. She didn't even get a chance to fully step inside Ms. Kat's apartment before the loudest blast she ever heard deafened her ears while the impact of the explosion so close in proximity blew her straight through Ms. Kat's door all the way to her kitchen, damn near sending her through the kitchen wall.

****

King George had hurried up and sprinted to the Humvee. He wanted another round of this big red amazon bitch, but he had to pull it together because he couldn't allow himself to get caught slippin' and end up in the same place his main man Devell was at, or even worse. Playing with the notion why he didn't kill the bitch on the spot made him question whether or not he's getting soft. That's when he pulled out the detonator to the explosive bomb he had left on her couch, gave the good pussy bitch one last thought, and pressed the button. In a matter of seconds he heard the blast as the bomb exploded, knowing from previous experiences that whatever the target was, it was a done deal.

"BOOOOOOM!!" was the sweet sound as he put the Humvee in drive and slid back through the path, back past the bank, jumping onto State Road 540 heading back towards the hospital's way to check on his main man, hoping he's came to so he can get him out of Winter Haven and up to the Big Apple State with him.

Chapter 23

Big-O had done called the number he received earlier from the broad at the hospital. He knew that He was treading on thin waters but right now he really didn't give a fuck. he was on his own, his big homie had made it clear of that and he knew Devell didn't fuck with him coming or going, so he felt like why should he respect him on any level. "This nigga know the motto. Slippers don't count! And he was about to show his ass that he slipped all the way up by letting me get my hands on his bitch!" thought Big-O. He didn't have any transportation and he damn sho' wasn't about to be escorted around in a fucking cab so he had Tarrell to come and pick him up, which she didn't hesitate doing.

After about twenty minutes, she had pulled up to the Hampton Inn, parking by the side exit door in her baby blue beamer. It wasn't no Rolls Royce, but it was hers. She didn't have any payments. Devell bought it for her when they got together, mainly because he didn't want her driving his shit and he needed the car for a lil dipper anyways when he made drug runs. But right now, she was going to see another nigga in the car her man had got her while he was laid up in a hospital fighting for his life. She had hit him back on his cell to let him know she was there and if he wanted a ride back to the hospital he better hurry his ass up.

Big-O let her know it will be about ten to fifteen minutes and asked her if she didn't mind coming up. She agreed and made it up to his room. She never been to the Hampton's, but the elevator ride made her wish this was her permanent residence. When she made it to the room, she let herself in just like he had asked her to do. Tarrell couldn't believe how magnificent the room was, it looked to be bigger than her house.

"What's up with you?" said Big-O as he greeted her.

"Nothing much...this is a very nice room. It must be expensive!" Tarrell said as she stared into Big-O's massiveness. He had on a pair of grayish looking Diesel jeans, some black rugged Timberland boots and a white wife beater. Tarrell was able to see all the tattoos that covered his arms and top part of his chest that the tank top couldn't cover up. He had his diamond ear ring in and had just finished polishing up his eight gold teeth he had at the top of his mouth.

Tarrell walked all the way across the room to the window to see the sky view, the room had a perfect setting of Lake Ned. Even though it was late, she was still able to see the participants come in from the lake on their jet skis and power boats. It was amazing how the setting illuminated on the lake's ripple from the way the lighting was prepared outside. Tarrell just stood there lost in admiration as she felt someone's hand grope her from the back. She immediately got offensive as she snatched away.

"Nigga, what the fuck is you doing? My nigga don't play that shit. And besides, I thought you were his friend!" said Tarrell.

"Nah baby girl, you're wrong. I don't fuck with that nigga and he don't fuck with me!" said Big-O letting it be made clear. After what King George had said, talking about; I should have let Devell kill your ass years ago was all it took. Now it was "Fuck Devell and whoever else!" to him.

"Well, why was you at the hospital?" she asked.

"Because of the big homie. But it's fuck that nigga too right now!"

"So why did you call me to come and get you and take you back to the hospital?"

"I just said that to get you here." said Big-O as he stood in front of Tarrell while she stood facing him with her back to the scenic view she was just enjoying.

"So, why did you want me here? You already know I belong to someone else."

"Yea, you're right. But I can tell you're not happy!"

"And what makes you think that I'm not happy?" she asked, because this nigga was reading her off like a book.

"First, the way you was looking at me when we first showed up at the hospital. Then the little conversation we shared when we had a few moments to ourselves. And not to mention, you gave me your phone number."

"I thought you were his friend! That's why I gave you my number, but I see that was a terrible mistake."

"Baby girl, the eyes don't lie, they never do. Like right now, they're telling me the same thing they did at the hospital!"

"And what's that?" she asked as her breathing began to get heavier by the seconds.

"That you want me, and that you wonder if I can keep us a secret. Am I right?"

"And what if you are?" she asked seductively, batting her long eye lashes at him as if she was a butterfly. That's all it took for Big-O. He was so easy to be seduced, and now here he was about to violate the most sacred rule in the game; don't fuck with another nigga's bitch or family.

As Big-O moved in closer, taking the one step that it took to seal their bodies together as if they were one. He gently wrapped his arms around her and gripped her butt. She didn't have much ass to work with. To be honest, she didn't have no ass. Her main asset was her 36 triple D's and her greenish brown eyes. Also, she had some long ass hair that was all hers. She was five foot nine, and had to look up at Big-O who towered over her at six foot four. He lifted her up into his embrace by her butt so she was eye level with him. She couldn't even resist any longer. As much as she wanted to fight him and play hard to get, a big and strong man was her weakness. As Big-O leaned in to kiss her, she already had her mouth open anticipating the moment. Their tongues met and sent vibrations through both of their bodies as they kissed for a few minutes, until both of their comfort levels were at ease. Pulling back, Big-O asked Tarrell..."Let's fuck!"

She was horny, but she wasn't about to let another nigga fuck her. Only Devell's dick was going up inside of her. "Nawl, big sexy ass nigga! That'll be moving a little too fast, don't you think so?" Replied Tarrell to his advances.

"I mean, if we're going to fuck around later what difference would it make?" said Big-O trying to plead his case for some pussy.

"I'll tell you what! We ain't fucking, so get that out of your mind. But what I will do is suck your dick!"

"Yea, alright then!" complied Big-O really not a fan of getting head, but he was in heat right now. That lil episode with the bitch Pumpkin was still present in his mind, and he was ready for another round.

Big-O just stood there, looking at Tarrell like; *Bitch, what's the hold up?* She caught on quick and didn't waste another second as she reached into the middle section of his jeans, undoing the buttons as the heavy duty Diesel jeans hit the floor, still wrapped around his ankles. Tarrell was a pro when it came to sucking a dick, well at least that's what she thought. But when she reached inside Big-O's boxer briefs, she wasn't too thrilled with what she pulled out. Never in her life did she ever have a dick this small in her mouth, ass or pussy. She use to blast her home girls when they use to come running back stressing their man wasn't packing. They even came up with a name for niggas that had little dicks. They called them "Fun Size." And that's what she held in her hand at the moment, a fun size dick.

She wrapped her whole hand around his shit and it disappeared. She almost bust out laughing but she kept her composure and rubbed the head of his dick with the palm of her right hand. Once she got him semi hard, she dropped down to her knees and damn near swallowed his whole dick, nuts and all. She was determined to suck this little dick right off the nigga body. Big-O was never able to get into the mood for head with any bitch he ever fucked with. Hell, his dick never got a full erection during head before. At least until now, because whatever trick this bitch had did with her hands, rubbing it across his dick head, he felt his shit began to stiffen up.

"Oh shit! This bitch might have the magic touch!" thought Big-O as he anticipated her next move when she damn near swallowed him whole and flew her tongue across his dick, flicking it like a race car while she kept all of him buried down her throat. Big-O damn near took flight through the ceiling as he stood on his toes, all the way to his toe nails.

"Oh shit, now that's what I'm talking 'bout!" moaned Big-O as he looked down to watch this bitch perform magic with her mouth, lips, and tongue. Tarrell wasn't faking with him either. She sucked his dick from every angle possible. Being that he was part of the itty-bitty committee, it made sucking his dick much more easier. She was able to pop her throat with his dick, jaw bone the dick, cuff his nuts with her tongue while she sucked his ass dry. Hell, Tarrell was just trying shit because she could and knew she had this big ass nigga about to blow a fuse. Big-O was only moments away from filling her mouth up with his sweet cum and wasn't about to warn her at all. He wanted to see this bitch face when he nutted all in her shit. He tried to hold on as best he could but this bitch was just too much for him. Big-O started to grunt, grabbing her by the ear as his body over powered his will and released every bit of semen he had stored inside of his nut sack.

Holding his head back as he stared into the ceiling, he let out a big grunt as he kept her ear locked in his left hand with a death grip, not knowing he had done dug a hole in her ear all the way to the white meat. Tarrell didn't even feel it, she was zoned out. When it came to sucking dick she allowed nothing and no one to distract her. Getting up off her knees she kept Big-O's little dissolved dick in her hand as she squeezed it, demanding his attention. As soon as he brung his head down from the la-la land he was lost in, she leaned in and stuck her tongue in Big-O's mouth making him lock lips with her. She still had some of his cum in her mouth, she knew what she was about to do could cost her a major beat down or even her life. But, she had to try him as she spit the cum out of her mouth straight into his mouth. Tarrell couldn't believe it as Big-O swallowed all the cum she had spit into his mouth. She leaned back and was like, "You're nasty for real!" giggling the words out.

"Shit, it's mines!" he said releasing his embrace, letting Tarrell step back a few steps. He turned towards the bed where he had piles of money at and started putting the bundles into his duffle bag.

"Damn, where did you get all of this money from?" asked Tarrell, just now seeing all the cash this nigga had all over the bed. If she would've noticed it at first, she would've put that pussy on his ass and fucked him into a coma and got missing with it all!" she thought to herself.

"Just a few dollars I brought with me to have some fun!" said Big-O, trying to talk like he really lived that boss life. Hell, he done saw King George stunt so hard he knew exactly how to do it. All he had to do was act like his big homie.

"How much is there?" Asked Tarrell all nosey. Never in her life has she witnessed that much money. Devell never had that much.

"That's two million dollars, cash!"

"Are you serious? You mean to tell me that's two million dollars and it's all yours?"

"You damn right it is. Why, you want to touch it?" asked Big-O, wanting to fuck with the bitch head for a second.

"Hell yea!"

Tarrell rushed the bed and dived onto the remaining bundles that were left, making them spread out like a pond of water. Spreading her arms and legs out, flapping them up and down as if she was making snow angels. Big-O was dying laughing. He knew he had this animal bitch where he wanted her, and he had plans to fuck her all the way over when the time presented itself.

"Alright, play time over with. I'm ready to roll!" said Big-O, wanting to get out and spend some of his new found riches.

Tarrell stopped making angels and looked up at him wondering what the fuck he meant talking bout; I'm ready to roll.

"Where you going? Because if you're rolling with me, I'm heading back to the hospital where my man at!"

"Bitch, I ain't going to no damn hospital. Fuck that hospital and fuck your nigga. I ain't on that fake shit." said Big-O as he started to display a little anger. "And get the fuck up!" he continued, pushing Tarrell ass off the bed as he gathered all of the scattered bills up and neatly packed them into the duffle bag with the rest of the money.

"Damn nigga, what the fuck you mad for? I just sucked your dick! What else you want from me? My nigga is fighting for his life and I should be there right by his side." said Tarrell sternly.

"I said what I had to say, and you ain't going back to that nigga either! Fuck that nigga, I hope he die! Bitch you're mines now, so let's go."

Tarrell was lost for words, she wanted to read this nigga and curse his ass out something nasty, but, something inside of her wouldn't let her. In reality, everything about him turned her on, especially the hatred he had for her man. This was a major decision for her, because ain't no way in hell she was going to let this nigga get away with all that money and she didn't get her share.

"So, where are you going daddy?" said Tarrell as she decided to ride with this nigga, if only for the moment.

Picking up his bezzled out Cartier watch, Big-O checked the time. It was 7:20 pm, plenty of time to bust a move.

"Let's hit up the mall right quick, I don't have any gear down here and since I'm here to stay, I have to pick up a few things." iterated Big-O, happy now that he's finally able to see what it feels like to buy the mall out. He only had about three hours to do so, but he felt that was enough time to blow at least twenty thousand dollars.

"I know you're going to buy me something, right?"

"Yeah, let's get the fuck out of here!"

"Okay daddy!" mocked Tarrell as she headed towards the door, looking back over her shoulder to see if this nigga was following suit, which he was. He had the oversized duffle bag on his shoulder while he pulled the carry on suit case he had all of his personal shit in. Big-O wasn't planning on coming back to the room, even though it was paid up for a whole week. He had plans to grab him his own spot tomorrow.

Looking back to make sure he got everything he needed, he saw the custom Deep Vision suit laid across the counter top. "Fuck that dressing up shit. I'm back at the crib, it's time to turn the fuck up for real!" he thought closing the door behind himself as he followed Tarrell to the elevator all the way down to the parking lot, where she had her BMW parked.

"This is your car? What the fuck is this?" barked Big-O.

"This my baby! What, you don't like it?" asked Tarrell.

"Hell fuck nawl, it's too fucking small!"

"Well, buy me another car! Until then, get your ass in and let's go." said Tarrell trying to establish some ground in this fake ass relationship she had done obligated herself to. I guessed it worked because Big-O just shut the fuck up and got in the car after putting his suit case in the trunk and the duffle bag full of money onto the back seat. Adjusting the seat to his liking, so he'd have enough leg room, Big-O released the seats lock, making it slide all the way back as he reclined the top part as well.

"So, which mall you wanna go to?"

"Whichever one is the closest!"

"That would be Eagle Ridge Mall on 27."

"I never been there, do they have hip hop clothes stores?" asked Big-O because what he heard about Eagle Ridge Mall was that it was for old peoples.

"Hell yea, they got everything in there, just like Lakeland Mall. But I think Eagle Ridge Mall is a little better!"

"What make you think that?" asked Big-O knowing first hand Lakeland Mall was the hottest spot to grab wear and fresh kicks out of in Polk County.

"You'll see for yourself. But you gotta hit this store up called "Re-Up" It's a hip-hop fashion store with all the latest shit no other store has." bragged Tarrell.

"That sound like it's my type of spot! Wake me up when we get there." said Big-O. Not two seconds later he was snoring his ass off.

One thing Tarrell knew how to do, that was spend some fucking money. She was already on a ten thousand dollar a month allowance that Devell gave her to handle all the bills with and blow the rest, which she did with ease each and every month. She knew exactly what she wanted. She was just in Re-Up the other day trying on the new Derion stretch body jean outfit.

"I'm gonna make this nigga buy me the outfit, the

shoes, the bag, and some accessories." thought Tarrell to herself as she pushed the Beamer coupe as fast as she could towards Eagle Ridge Mall.

Chapter 24

Homicide Detective Grant had put the briefing together just as the Captain had asked him to do. The room was full of chatter. Damn near every cop in the precinct was there, except the ones that was out patrolling. All the plain clothes officers, detectives from every division, as well as Internal Affairs. They were ready for the mandatory debriefing Detective Grant had summoned as everyone watched him and Officer Hernandez chop it up about how something had seemed wrong when he last saw Officer Fulwiley.

"Everything is playing so clear to me Detective!" said Officer Hernandez. "Usually when I talk about sports with him he'll get all excited and tell me how his Spurs defeated my Heat in the Championship Finals. But instead, he was acting paranoid as hell. His car was parked, slammed up against the garage entrance if I'm not mistaken. And, he said something about his sister was missing again, whatever that meant!"

"His sister was missing!" replied Detective Grant

incredulously, knowing damn well Fulwiley didn't even have a sister. All of that was a made up lie.

"Yea, he said his sister!"

"That bastard doesn't have a fucking sister, all of that is make believe!"

"You know what! I was questioning that myself because none of that shit came across my radio." said Officer Hernandez. And before they could continue with the conversation the Captain entered the room.

Captain Cheryl Wertz was every one of their fantasy fucks, but not one single officer at the department has been able to bone her. At least not that anybody else knew of. But that didn't stop them from trying. She stayed the topic of conversation for every male counterpart there, both single and married. Captain Wertz were a prize jewel, even the women officers wanted some of her. It was so much money betted on who would get lucky first, before long they'd have to bet all that money towards something else.

At five foot seven, weighing 165 pounds, Captain Wertz was way more prepared to fight crime than what her measurements perceived her to be. She had a 38 triple D size breast, a 26 inch waist, and a 45 inch spread where anyone that had anything to think with knew that's where the majority of her weight came from. The conference room was as quiet as a Christmas mouse when Captain Wertz took the podium.

"Um Um Um!" was the sound that blared through the speaker as the captain cleared her throat. "Hello everyone, and thanks to all of you for gathering at such short notice. I'm assuming that all of you are aware of the recent events that's led up to this briefing. Am I correct?" everybody agreed by shaking their heads up and down in unison.

"Well, I'm here to tell everyone that I've reviewed the tape and that me and the Attorney General's Office had conducted a thorough investigation regarding Officer Fulwiley's erratic and rogue behavior." Said the captain as one of her officers blurted out, cutting her short.

"What is it to brief about? We all saw the video and it's plain and simple that Officer Fulwiley is harboring potential murder suspects. I say we put an all-out man hunt for this criminal imposing as an officer of the law."

"YEAH!" erupted the room to the officer's truth as the rest of his counterparts cheered him on.

"Calm down everyone. This is not the time to be voicing opinions, playing judge and juror. I've already sent the charging information to the Attorney General's Office. It's no longer in our hands."

"So what about the murder investigation?" blurted out Homicide Detective Grant.

"That is no longer our concern as well. It's been administered to the Federal authority as well, this case is closed. Whatever evidence you gathered in this investigation will be immediately turned over to the F.B.I. Special Agent Owens."

"How is you going to turn over my investigation and don't confirm it with me?" asked Detective Grant.

"That's all I have to share at this moment. If anyone has a problem with the way this situation was handled then I recommend you file an insubordinate report with Internal Affairs." pausing for a second to scan the room, wanting to get a good look at everybody who had smoke to blow towards her decision just in case she had to do some rearranging. It didn't take long either, one quick glance and all the back and forth chatter was ceased. Nobody wanted any part of the Captain's wrath.

"This meeting's adjourned!" said the Captain as she stared Homicide Detective Grant down as he abruptly exited the room.

"The Feds my ass!" thought Detective Grant to himself as he rushed to his office, gathering together all the info and evidence he'd received from the murder scene, placing it into his office safe. "Ain't no way in hell I'm going to let these blood thirsty muthafucka's come in and solve my case. I'll show them who the fuck I am."

****

Old Man Larry had left Joann to look after Tenille and K-Boy while he ran to get them something to eat knowing them niggas had to be starving because the hospital food don't be hitting on shit. He swung by McDonalds and tore their dollar menu down. Larry brought everything from burgers to fries, chicken nuggets, fish sandwiches, and their famous apple pie. The food run didn't take but about thirty minutes. The McDonalds was only a quarter mile down the road from the LaQuinta where they were at.

Joann had heard when the van pulled up. She peeped out of the window and it was her baby Larry as she suspected. Larry had his hands full, trying to tote all the bags of food, as well as the drinks. Joann hurried up and opened the door, knowing her man too damn well. Larry was going to try and open the door with his hands full.

"Hold up baby...let me help you with that!" yelled Joann, not wanting Larry to drop or waste anything. Hell, she was hungry as a muthafucka herself.

"What you got baby?" asked Joann, grabbing the drinks out of his right hand.

"I got everything!"

"Did you get me some Checkers, baby? You know how much I love me some Checkers."

"Nah baby doll, I didn't make no Checkers run. Everything is from McDonalds." Larry said as a moment of silence serenaded the room's atmosphere before he interrupted, "Baby if you need me to go back out and get you something from Checkers I will. I just didn't want to go too far out knowing the circumstances at hand."

"Yea, you're right baby. And I'm sorry for acting up!" Joann pleaded. "Just give me something to eat because I'm starving!"

"Hell yea, I'm starving like a muthafucka too!" said K-Boy as Tenille just shook his head in agreement as well. They were all hungry as hell. As soon as Old Man Larry put the bags of food down it wasn't seconds before they devoured everything there. Joann was sharing the last apple pie with Larry when Tenille forced himself to speak.

"Who did this to me, Old Skool?" he asked.

Larry sighed deeply before he chose his next words, "Listen young soldier, what I'm about to put before you isn't all factual. It's all hearsay, but I'm obliged to share with you all that's been brought to my attention!" said Larry knowing these two gangstas in front of him had no clue what happened to them and their friends.

"Please Old Skool, just tell us what you know!" begged Tenille, almost about to cry as his eyes watered up keeping his attention on Larry as the old gangsta shook his head side to side revealing something terrible has happened just from his body language.

"Whoever came up in your spot left y'all for dead. When I came through the door I spotted you; pointing at K-Boy, on the floor. I checked your pulse to see if you had a living chance and as bad as it looked, you had a pulse. You was holding on for dear life. I checked the next nigga and he was dead as a muthafucka."

"Who?" asked K-Boy.

"The skinny big head one who thinks he's the coolest person alive!" and right then K-Boy knew he was talking about Malcolm, his childhood friend. He couldn't control his emotions as he let out a cry that had so much hurt in it.

"NOOOOOOOOO!" he turned to face his cousin Tenille knowing he knew exactly who Larry was talking about as well. But all he saw was a coldness in his stare that he didn't see since their robbing days. A look he thought he'd never witness again. Regaining his composure, K-Boy asked Old Man Larry to finish telling them what all he knew.

"Once I saw that K-Boy was alive, I wondered if there was any other people alive in the house, so I rushed through to the back to check the rooms and I see three more bodies. The hallway was kind of dark, but I was able to recognize you; Larry pointing at Tenille, shot the fuck up, laid there slumped over the other two bodies. I checked all of y'all pulses and out of the three, you was the only one hanging in there fighting for your life. I got my lady here to pull my pick-up to the door and I loaded you two on the back and rushed y'all to the Brandon Medical Center, and now we're here!"

"Give us a name! Did anybody get to see who it was?" asked K-Boy.

"Nah, not that I know of. The nigga that fled the scene supposedly had on a ski mask."

"Oh yea, so a nigga came to wipe us out for good, huh?" thought K-Boy as he damn near blew his brain up trying to figure out who the fuck would want to kill any one of them. They'd been left that gangsta shit alone years ago and been trapping that dope money.

K-Boy probably didn't know what the fuck happened, but as the seconds passed Tenille's memory began to come back as clear as the blue sky. The only thing he couldn't make out was the face on the trigger man. He lost three soldiers, and damn near got killed himself. All Tenille could think of was them ten bricks he just took a lost for. K-Boy needed to know more, he felt it was something else that somebody knew and wasn't telling them.

"Anything else Old Skool? I mean, is there anything you could think of that you haven't told us yet?"

"Not that I can recall!"

"Just think for a second and be sure."

"You know what! Since you said that, they did hit me up asking about a burgundy car on some big rims."

"Who the fuck has a burgundy car?" K-Boy asked

himself as he patted his foot on the floor as if there was a prize for the answer.

"Where did they spot this car at? And what kind of car was it?" asked Tenille.

"They say they seen it on Spirit Lake Road, coming from Bartow right before Polk County Sheriff found the stolen Dodge Ram that the nigga who hit y'all up had used.

"Winter Haven! Who the fuck from Winter Haven got a burgundy car on big rims?" mumbled K-Boy as he looked at Tenille, hoping he'd come up with an answer.

"And what kind of car you said it was?" asked K-Boy.

"They said..." and before Larry could finish, K-Boy interrupted.

"Hold up, tell me who the fuck they is first. At least I'd know if the information is valid or a muthafucka just running their mouth."

"Nah young soldier, this info from my fam and when they say something, that shit's official." clarified Old Man Larry.

"Okay then, tell us the rest you know Old Skool."

"As I was saying, they said it was one of those new town cars, a Lincoln or something with the spinning rims."

Everybody paused for a moment, especially Tenille and K-Boy. They knew exactly who this car belonged to. But Larry and Joann was stuck looking at how K-Boy and Tenille face had dropped.

"What's up soldier, y'all know who this nigga is?" asked Larry, "Because if y'all do, we're going to have to hit this nigga hard and quick. Especially if he finds out you two are still alive.

Tenille knew Old Man Larry was right, but he also knew that this nigga wasn't to be played with and if they rolled up slippin' then they all could be dead for real and Tenille wasn't trying to go out like no sucka. His mind was racing a hundred miles an hour as he tried to figure out why he chose to hit his spot. "I thought me and the nigga was cool!" and that's when it dawned on him...TINY. they both was fucking with her and she must've told him what he had said, remembering clearly when he told her that the nigga wasn't a hustla, all he do is rob niggas.

"DAMNNNN!!!!!!!" was all Tenille could say in agony as he tried to deal with the realization that Devell had put out a price on his head, one that he knew Devell would cash in on with his very own hands.

Chapter 25

Another day had come and gone. Big-O was enjoying his new found fame. He had tore the stores down in the mall last night with what little time he had to shop being that it was already late. He was still determined to spend some money, and he did. When Mr. Tony at Re-Up Fashions saw the piles of money that Big-O had to spend, he laid out the red carpet. Mr. Tony pulled out new arrival shit that he wasn't planning on putting out until next week. Mr. Tony saw Big-O's weakness and went after it. He catered to Tarrell's every desire, busting open box after box. She was decked out in the latest and hottest urban gear around, marching back and forth from the dressing room like she was one of America's Next Top Model's.

Big-O blew seventeen thousand dollars last night in less than an hour. At first Tarrell was hesitant about giving Big-O some pussy, but after seeing how he spent so much attention on her as well as his money, she had plans on fucking this nigga to death...and she did. She knew from when she had given him head at the hotel that he wasn't packing much so she had to be in complete control if she even stood a chance climaxing off this nigga. Big-O tried to eat her pussy and she was enjoying it. The head was so good she couldn't stand it any longer, she needed to feel something hard inside of her. Even if it wasn't much, it was enough.

Tarrell straddled Big-O and grinded him as if she was having a seizure. After she nutted multiple times, she laid on top of him facing the opposite direction in the sixty-nine as they sucked each other dry. When they were finally finished, they both had done passed out in Tarrell's king size bed that the only man she ever shared it with was Devell. Well, you can say Pumpkin, but that was different. She was violating every law there was to break as far as dealing with morals of a relationship. Big-O wanted to go to the car lot when he awoke, he needed to cop him a whip and it had to be something super fat. He was about to make a statement, one that people will remember forever.

They both awoke around 10:am Tarrell nor Big-O took a shower. They both got dressed and hit the highway, heading for the car lot. Tarrell was just as excited herself, she was going to try and get her a new car out of the deal as well. Even if it was just a used car, at least something different than the one she had right now. It was 11:53am when Tarrell and Big-O pulled into the Mercedes Benz dealership in Orlando off of Colonial Boulevard. Big-O already knew what it was he wanted, he just hope this particular dealership carried that make and model. As soon as they exited Tarrell's baby blue beamer, they were greeted by a short, frail, and fragile looking Indian man who also looked to have had a series of facial cosmetic surgeries.

"Hello folks, how may I help you two lovely people today?" asked the funny face man.

Big-O hated when people tried to talk all intelligent towards him, like he was slow. He made it his priority to be rude and obnoxious whenever he encountered such an event, like the one he was in now.

"Listen to me you Olive Oil looking muthafucka, I'm not trying to be your muthafucking friend, so save all that buttery talk for somebody else. Where is the fucking owner of this place before I find another dealership to spend my money at." barked Big-O, making the little guy damn near deny he was the owner of the Mercedes Benz dealership, except for two reasons. "One, business was slow, and two, he knew this big ape wasn't qualified to have any bank approve him for a loan, so he had to have cash and lots of it if he wanted to move anything off of this lot." thought the owner as he regained his balls knowing the leverage was in his hands now, and he was about to show this brute of a man how powerful he really was.

"Excuse me, I beg your pardon sir! First I would like to correct you. There's no person by the name of Olive Oil that's employed at this establishment. If you desire to purchase any of the fine automobiles here, then you will refrain from using such atrocious language. Now, if I made myself clear, is there anything in particular you had in mind?" said the Indian looking man, scared out of his wits knowing this giant could break him in half with ease.

Big-O couldn't believe what he was hearing. He killed people for lesser shit and here this toothpick looking muthafucka was talking to him like he wasn't shit. He had to think, and he had to think smartly. He was on his own now and he knew the least mistake could cost him dearly. King George wasn't around to help fix his fuck-ups anymore. And not to mention, he wasn't about to leave without the car of his dreams.

"Ha Ha Ha!" Laughed Big-O, trying to down play the little Indian guy's demands, not wanting to show any sign of weakness in front of his new bitch Tarrell.

"I'm here for one car and one car only. The new Mercedes Benz S600 Maybach!" exclaimed Big-O as him and the owner locked eyes. This particular dealership was the only one that carried this new model of Mercedes and hasn't yet been able to sell one to anybody. Now, here this street thug stood in front of him inquiring about a two hundred, thirty thousand dollar car. The little Indian guy's face lit up. He knew the power he held in this particular request. He had plans on jacking the price all the way up past the sticker price.

"As a matter of fact, I do have that vehicle. I hope you like white because that's the only color we have, and as a matter of fact I'm the only dealer in the whole Central Florida area that has this model Mercedes in stock." said the owner as he watched this thug impersonator light up with excitement as he turned around and grabbed an oversized duffle bag out of the back seat of the B.M.W. they came screeching up in. Just seeing the large duffle bag, it transformed the owner into something he was most familiar with; a certified salesman.

"Sir, if you would like to view this beautiful car, then follow me." said the owner as he led Big-O and Tarrell inside the spacious Mercedes Benz dealership, right over to the showroom floor. You could tell the little Indian was a master at this. As they got into eye sight of the massive, beautiful, and powerful machine, he started running down the specifics like he had them memorized for just this occasion.

"This vehicle is a 2017. As you can tell, it is the all-new Mercedes Benz S600-Maybach. It has a twin turbo V-12 supercharged engine instead of the standard V-8. This particular vehicle is fully loaded with every luxury amenity available. Such as; reclining rear seats that has its own heat and cooling system. The paint is the only white in its existence, Snow White Diamond Pearl with triple diamond stitch snow white leather. And it has that baller swag you guys look for with the custom twenty-two inch factory rims and low profile tires."

While the little frail man kept on blabbering about how bad the car was, Big-O had done sat inside and went to adjusting the seats like the car was already his. It didn't take Tarrell long as she caught on and joined Big-O adjusting the passenger seat, knowing that was her seat and hers only. If she was leaving her nigga, then it wasn't no way on earth this nigga was getting out of her sight.

"So, what do you think? Isn't it a beauty?" stated the owner, hoping he had buttered this potential buyer up thinking about the large portion of cash that he possibly could receive.

"Let's cut the chase man. How much is this car?" asked Big-O, ready to get the fuck on so he can stunt in his new Benz Maybach.

"Why don't we go inside my office!" inquired the owner.

"Now we're talking!" responded Big-O as he snatched the duffle bag up off the hood, following the owner into his office which was a see through glass partition that sat dead in the center of the dealership's main floor. Before Big-O could close the door behind himself, Tarrell came squeezing in right behind him.

"Don't leave me baby!" she said, trying to talk all sweet and shit, hoping to get a car as well.

"While I see if I can find a bank to finance you, I'm going to need you to fill out these forms."

"Hold up, I'm not trying to fill out shit, and I don't need a bank to finance me for a fuck thang. I'm trying to buy the car with cash money, or is it you don't take cash?" asked Big-O, teasing his ass, knowing damn well everybody in the world took cash.

The owner knew by the look of everything that this was going to be a straight cash transaction. He just needed to get it verified.

"So, what's the price?" Big-O asked.

"Being that you're paying in cash, that's a seven percent deduction on the total cost. Just give me a second as I add up these numbers." said the owner grabbing the calculator, forgetting about the original sticker two hundred and thirty-thousand-dollar sticker price and jumped straight to the ceiling.

"You want the show room floor model, fully loaded! That's two hundred and ninety thousand dollars, minus the seven percent discount, which is twenty thousand dollars, leaving a total balance of two hundred and sixty nine thousand dollars...cash!"

Big-O didn't even hesitate. He saw his big homie stunt like this so many times, dropping cash on everything he bought. Not leaving any paper trails. Big-O had the money in ten thousand dollar stacks. He opened the bag up and went to stacking the stacks on the owner's desk. When he finished, it was twenty seven of the stacks neatly placed on the desk.

"Now where my fucking keys at?!" barked Big-O.

"Please, give me a moment while I get your car placed outside and ready for you. And by the way, who would you like to have your new car registered to?" Asked the owner.

"Oh, um...put it in!" trying to think of somebody to put the car in their name, Big-O just settled on using himself. "Put it in Otis Richardson!" said Big-O as he looked over at Tarrell, who looked like she just got slapped with an ugly stick with her mouth all balled up and arms folded across her breast.

"Damn baby girl, what's wrong with you?" asked Big-O.

"I WANT A CAR TOO!!!" pleaded Tarrell, batting her eyes, trying to display her puppy face.

"So what, you want me to pick it out for you as well?" s*tated Big-O as he continued, "You better hurry up because I'm trying to bust a move and put some shoes on this bitch!"

Tarrell knew exactly what that meant. Every nigga she knew that referred to; putting shoes on a car meant rims. And she wanted in on everything. Here she was running around with a nigga that didn't even like her man. But what was fucked up, Devell was in the hospital fighting for his life and she knew she was supposed to be right there at his side. *"Oh well, what's done is done. It wasn't any turning back now, she was all in!"* thought Tarrell before she told Big-O what car she wanted.

"Right there baby!" she said Pointing in the direction of a few Benz coupes.

"Right where?" Big-O replied as he followed the direction of her hand noticing a powder blue, two door CL500 hard top and a blood red, long nose SL550 convertible Benz that looked like it had a wide body kit already on it.

"Right there baby, the red one...that's the one I want!"

Tarrell had so much enthusiasm running through her body she didn't know how to act, she did everything in her body to stop from jumping out of her chair.

"Oh yea! That's a bad ass car right there. How much is that red two door Benz?" asked Big-O, ready to pay for it and get the hell out of there.

"That's the new 2017 SL550 AMG Benz coupe." said the little Indian before he was rudely interrupted by Big-O.

"I don't care about all that! She said she want the red one, then that's what she gets. Now, how much for the car?"

Having already bust his head on the Maybach for over forty-six thousand more than the car actually cost. He had contemplated on selling the SL at sticker price, but the rude way he was being addressed at the moment made what little thought he had being fair vanish.

"You're right sir, that particular car cost three hundred and fifty thousand dollars, minus the seven percent for cash purchase will leave a total balance of three hundred twenty five thousand dollars." said the owner as he thought about the eighty five thousand and change he made over charging this big dumb ass nigga.

Big-O quickly piled three stacks on the desk beside the already twenty seven stacks and left Tarrell there to put her own car in whatever name she wanted to put it in. With the duffle bag strapped to his shoulder, Big-O headed over to his new white Mercedes as he watched the assembly crew dismantle the large window frames, opening up a section in the floor-to-ceiling windows, making the building open up like a large garage.

"So, that's how they get the cars in and out!" said Big-O to himself as he watched one of the workers drive his Maybach out of the building. Once outside, the driver handed over a double set of keys to Big-O leaving him alone with his new car. Big-O didn't waste any time. He immediately got inside, closed the door and threw the duffle bag on the back seat as he started the car.

Big-O couldn't believe it. Here it was, he had his first car and it was a Maybach. He turned on the A.C. and pulled the beautiful space ship around to the front where Tarrell's two door 650i was. He didn't leave anything in her car. All the clothes he bought last night was still at her house, but he still got out and went inside of her Beamer in search of some music. He needed something gutter to listen to and he already knew she had that gutter shit. That's all she's been playing since yesterday. He grabbed a Trick Daddy mix tape and as he was getting back out he heard a menacing growl; VRRRRRMMMMM!!, that stole his attention. As soon as he turned to witness where the powerful sound came from, he saw it was Tarrell pulling up in her new car.

"You ready?" she asked.

"Yea, I'm ready. But what are you going to do about this car?" asked Big-O.

"Fuck that car! I'm in my car. Let me get my purse and C.D.'s." she said getting out racing through her old car getting what was most important to her. She had sold the car to the dealership for a stack and wasn't even thinking about looking back. All the money this nigga had, she was going to try to get him to buy her a new house.

"Alright, let's go baby. I'm following you now!" said Tarrell as she idled the supercharged motor waiting on Big-O to lead her wherever he wanted to. She was officially all in.

Chapter 26

Officer Fulwiley was a complete wreck. He was under a Federal investigation that was in progress at the moment for his recent involvement in a criminal act, claiming he was the culprit in a kidnapping, harboring a fugitive, and negligence by an officer of the law. Fulwiley knew that if these accusations stood firm, it could cost him his freedom as well as life behind bars. Even though his relationship ties with the Captain was certain to buy him a little extra time, he needed to make every move he could possibly make putting all his priorities in place and first priority on his list was to get off the kilo of cocaine that he cuffed from the murder scene.

It wasn't even a day ago since he dropped the twins off, and now he was lost as he tried to remember where the fuck the area was where they lived. Wasting over an hour driving in circles, Officer Fulwiley had finally came to his senses and called the number the twins had given him for directions, catching someone on the second ring.

"Hello!" answered Chineir to the unknown caller.

"Yes, ummm. May I speak to Moneisha?!" asked Fulwiley not knowing exactly who number belonged to who, but he knew it belonged to one of them.

"I'm sorry, this isn't Moneisha's number, this is her sister Chineir. If you would like to leave a message, I'd be more than glad to make sure she gets it." replied Chineir not knowing if this call was important or just another call from one of the many niggas she met at the club and passed her fucking number off to.

"You'll do. This Officer Fulwiley from Polk County. I'm going to need you to give me directions back to where y'all live. I've somehow gotten myself lost!"

Everything went silent for a brief moment. Chineir didn't know what the fuck to say. Whether she should hang up on him or give him directions. He did say he needed directions, which meant he couldn't find them. But Chineir became more afraid when she thought about all he had to do was make her and Moneisha murder suspects, they were bound to be found. And besides, one of these broke, bad doing, and thirsty ass hoes wouldn't hesitate to tell on them. So she decided to give him the directions as well as the security code to the guarded gated community they lived in. When Officer Fulwiley described where he was coming from, off of highway 60, it was still a twenty minute stretch to where they lived in Riverview, if the traffic was fair.

Chineir was in total dismay, "Why was the police coming back so soon? It haven't been twenty four hours since he dropped them off." she thought, not wasting time calling Moneisha. She was on her third try as the call rung for about five or six times before the answering machine picked up, screeching her sister's voice through the phone; HELLO, THIS IS ME, YOUR GIRL MONEISHA. I'M SORRY THAT I'M UNABLE TO COME TO THE PHONE AT THE MOMENT, BUT IF YOU LEAVE YOUR NAME, YOUR NUMBER, AND A BRIEF MESSAGE, I'LL BE MORE THAN GLAD TO GET BACK WITH YOU. TAH TAH!!" BEEEEP.

"Mo, if you get this message please hurry up and come home. I'm so scared right now. That police from the other night is on his way back over here and I'm home alone. PPLLEEAASSEE hurry home. I'll see you soon, and I love you!" pleaded Chineir in her message she left her sister. Contemplating on getting the fuck out of there so she didn't have to face him alone. Chineir ran erratically throughout the house, putting together a quick survival bag that consisted of a few outfits, shoes, panties, bra's, toothpaste, toothbrush, and last but not least; her tampons. It was around that time of the month and she wasn't about to let her period catch her slippin'.

Chineir hated driving, but under the circumstances she had no other choice. She paused for a moment and took a second to reevaluate everything to make sure she was doing the right thing. Checking her black Derion velour, one piece jump suit she had on and her black and gold Derion Booties, she was ready to roll. Chineir dashed to the garage and jumped inside of her new Maserati Ghibli, which was a gift from her millionaire boyfriend, or sugar daddy for what it mattered. Chineir knew she was about to get something special when he had asked her what was her favorite color, but never in a thousand years she would have thought it was going to be a hundred thousand dollar car. If he wasn't married, the day he surprised her with the baby blue Maserati was the same day she would have married him and locked his rich white ass in so nobody else could ever get a piece of the pie.

Chineir loaded her bag onto the seat of the Maserati and crunk the super power sports sedan up as it growled, making the V-8, 540hp turbo charged engine make the inside of the garage sound like a massive explosion. She was fascinated by fast and powerful cars. Her and Moneisha's father was a mechanic that specialized in rebuilding engines which automatically made her a grease monkey. Her father had passed away when she was ten, but she continued to admire the beauty of powerful cars in remembrance of her father.

Chineir mashed the gas, idling the car up just to hear the rumble under her car's hood. All of that brought a smile to her face as well as a tingling sensation throughout her body.

"Okay, let's get it!" said Chineir out loud to herself as she threw on her Dolce and Gabana shades that damn near took up her whole face. Pressing the garage opener making the oversized gate come rolling up into the ceiling. Pulling out, Chineir had to slam on brakes as the same black on black Dodge Charger that brung her and her twin sister home from Polk County whipped up into the driveway blocking her path as they locked stares, wondering what's next.

****

Moneisha was at the University Mall with her new nigga, well at least that's what he thought he was. Moe wasn't into the good niggas, she wanted nothing less than a street nigga. Her motto was "NO LONG TERM COMMITMENTS!" and what nigga fit the bill better than a nigga living on the edge. The results were always the same, either one or two things was bound to happen; a jail cell or the grave yard.

So, while the nigga balled out of control, Moneisha hung around and got her piece of the pie. She made sure she helped every balling street nigga she came across help spend their money like it was no tomorrow, and right now she had the hottest nigga in Tampa caking her. "Bimp" aka "Mr. Untouchable" he was the strongest drug dealer in the city. If drugs was being sold and it didn't have his stamp on it, then whoever the seller was never sold drugs again, literally. Bimp's drug spots had been good for the week, as a matter of fact, they all brung in record numbers, steady building his empire beyond measure. He had picked Moneisha up about an hour ago in his Jaguar CX17, the new SUV that wasn't even available for purchase yet. But he had one and it was bad with the kandy apple green paint job, sitting on a set of twenty-eight inch chrome Diablo's. Moneisha stayed like an hour from the mall where they were, she was enjoying the shopping spree. She was getting it all. They had done made two trips to the SUV already and both of their arms and hands were full again as the shopping bags was stuffed with all the latest designer clothes. Moneisha wanted to catch a movie and spend as much time with Bimp as she could because she had something special up her sleeve, and didn't need him to deny her when she popped the question to his ass. That's why she needed to butter his ass up as much as possible. Bimp had refused the invite, he didn't mind spending time with her because Moneisha was a bad bitch, and he was really feeling her. But today he had to meet the plug, and he wasn't going to be late doing that for no one.

Once they finished shopping they headed back to Bimp's SUV. Once inside, Moneisha grabbed her Gucci purse off the back seat and went straight to her phone. She always left it in the car when she was out chilling with Bimp. She refused to have anybody fuck up her vibe.

She noticed there was sixteen missed calls. *"Damn, a bitch must be really trying to get at me!"* she thought as she scrolled through them all to see if any of them were of importance to her. "What the fuck do Chineir want?" she asked herself, seeing that her sister tried calling her six times and left a message as well. "Something has to be wrong, Chi-Chi don't call me like that. Hell, she barely call me period!" said Moe to herself as she listened to the message that her twin had left.

"Beep; message 16 of 16: Moe, if you get this message, please hurry up and come home. I'm scared right now. That police from the other night is on his way back over here and I'm home alone. PPLLEEAASSEE hurry home...I'll see you soon, and I love you. Beep; message 16 of 16 is complete." said the recording.

"Oh, hell naw, not my sister!" Moneisha immediately

became covered with fear as she tried frantically to call her back, but only to be sent to the voice mail. She tried calling her three more times before her attempts were interrupted by an incoming call. "Who the fuck is this?!" thought Moe, about to send whoever it was straight to the voice mail until she noticed it was Odell, making her answer his call with urgency in her voice.

"HELLO?!"

"Damn cuz, why the fuck you're sounding all tensed up and shit?" asked Odell, as he had a lil laughter in his voice, thinking he had interrupted one of Moneisha's fuck sessions.

"Cuz, where you at?" asked Moneisha as her voice pleaded with Odell, letting him know something was wrong.

"I'm like five minutes from the crib, why? What's wrong Moe?" asked Odell concernly.

"Please hurry up and get to the house, Chineir left me a message talking about the police who brung us home was back on his way there, and she's home alone. I don't trust that cop, and I'm out of the area so you need to get there as soon as you can and make sure that Chi-Chi is alright." pleaded Moneisha.

"Cuz, I'm on the gas right now, you need to try and get home too because we have to figure all of this shit out!"

"Alright, and Odell...don't do anything crazy!" warned Moneisha as she ended the call.

"What's up baby, is everything alright?" asked Bimp.

"Yea, just a little family problem that we fucked around and got ourselves into, but we'll have it fix soon."

said Moe as she did her best to down play the situation.

"Are you sure? Because you know I'm here for you if you need me."

"Yea, I'm sure baby...let's get something to eat because I'm super hungry, and you still have about an hour before your meeting."

Bimp just took a moment to look at her. He was fucked up about the bitch, but not fucked up enough to be late meeting up with the plug. When it came to his business, Bimp would betray the world, let alone a bitch that didn't bring not one dime to the table.

"Nah baby girl, that would be playing it too close. Maybe next time. You know my motto; Business before pleasure."

"Alright, but you have to promise me you'll make up for it!"

"Don't I always do?" said Bimp as he lustfully stared Moneisha down, knowing he had to be careful because fucking with a bitch like Moneisha could cause a nigga to lose everything, including his own life.

Chapter 27

Homicide Detective Grant wasn't feeling any of the shit that was taking place. First, with Officer Fulwiley's actions with the murder suspects. Then the Captain's actions talking about the investigation has been handed over to the Feds. Nothing was quite adding up, that's why Detective Grant decided to put together his own little task squad with his most reliable and sourceful officers at his agency. The same officers who aided and assisted him on numerous missions where there was blood shed and lives lost. Basically his own 'Goon Squad'. They were all Detectives and if you didn't know any different, you'd think they were all street niggas by their appearances.

Detective Grant had immediately set up a personal meeting with his goon squad shortly after the Captain had dismissed them from their briefing. Detective Grant had relayed the meeting would be at their secondary spot, which meant behind the old drive in movie theater off Havendale Blvd. Everybody had done made it there, the whole goon squad except for one person who had a habit of always being late. Ten minutes had done passed as he came rolling up in his new Cadillac Escalade, the 2016 model. His truck was a grayish looking color on a set of twenty-eight inch Lexani rims and tires. It was easy understood why they called him "Yella", he had that real light skinned complexion that was highly visible, even behind the dark tint on his SUV. All of them had fixed up hood whips, that's how they were able to infiltrate street niggas when they would set them up. It was a total of five of them. The leader was Homicide Detective Gerry Grant. Whenever he was on his fuckery, he drove a Dodge Charger, the 2015 SRT Hellcat. The fastest street legal production car ever built. It was also a smoke gray with the double black rally stripes across the hood and the trunk. It had black mobbed out tint and a set of all black twenty-six inch rims that coordinated with the car's color scheme.

You had Officer Cole, aka "Ken Cole", who thought he was a real gangsta. He drove a Donk, just like the drug dealers. A two-door burgundy 1975 Caprice Classic on some twenty-six-inch DUB Bellagio's. Ken Cole was six foot five, dark skinned and wore a low haircut. Medium build, with a sixteen pack of gold teeth in his mouth. It was because of Ken Cole that Detective Grant and the rest of their Goon Squad was under investigation, three work related homicides this year alone, and all committed by the badge.

The other two members of the Goon Squad were brothers, and they were as nasty as they can get. Shandel and Links, both Jamaican immigrants. Shandel was the youngest of the two at twenty-seven years old, and Links, who was thirty. They were damn near inseparable. They did everything together, from living in the same apartment, fucking with the same women, and even sharing the same car, a matte black Lexus IS350 with matching matte black twenty inch racing rims and tires. Shandel and Links had one common goal, and that was to save as much money as possible to send back to their native home land of Jamaica to make sure their family was straight and well taken care of on the poverty stricken island. Out of everybody on the Goon Squad, Detective Grant was more fond of the Jamaican brothers. Even though they were only deputies, they were more efficient than any of the others, as if their skills set made them trained assassins. And just the look of them, you'd know they was going to fuck you over.

Yella had parked behind Ken's Donk and got out, acting like he didn't have any worries in the world, with his gold plated detective badge hanging from around his neck, resting on top of his pot belly. The rest of the Goon Squad gave him a standing ovation as they clapped their hands to his arrival.

"Fuck y'all!" said Yella, knowing his buddies was trying to be funny about his tardiness.

"Alright, alright, alright y'all, let's get down to business!" s+

aid Detective Grant, regaining the squad's attention as they settled down to see what it was that Detective Grant had called this emergency meeting for.

"I know you are all wondering why I called the squad

together! Well, a lot of shit has hit the fan within the last twenty-four hours. As you all know, Captain Wertz has pulled the plug from under us and brung in the FBI for this multiple homicide at that drug dealer's spot. But, I know better, and each and every one of you muthafuckas should know better to..."

"What the fuck you mean we all should know better?" asked Yella, because he wasn't feeling this conversation at the moment.

"What I mean you big dummy is that, not for one minute do I think them cock sucking federal bastards is here for a homicide investigation. I went to squeezing Fulwiley's balls on abetting the only two suspects to this murder we had. The Captain knew she was supposed to have him arrested, but instead, he's put up somewhere and God knows where he has the suspects hiding."

"So what difference does it makes? Let the feds handle that shit if that's what the Captain want!" said Shandel, confused to the overwhelming interest Detective Grant had in this matter.

"It makes a whole lot of difference, there's something I didn't share with none of you because I couldn't afford nobody switching sides and helping Internal Affairs with the investigation they have on us for corruption and murder!"

"They got what on us? How in the hell! Why are you just now telling us?" blurted out Ken Cole.

"You know exactly why! The same reason they have us under investigation in the first place, some of you muthafuckas talk too fucking much. Word got around that it was us who was responsible for the execution style murders in Boggy that Mouse got framed for.

"UNDER INVESTIGATION!" screamed Yella, as his mind went to racing back and forth with a million 'what if's', especially 'what if they all ended up in prison'.

"Yea, you fucking moron, that's why I haven't had any jobs for us lately because I.A. assigned Officer Fulwiley to us, to see what he can find out. But I've been playing his ass real good, keeping him close enough to think they got the wrong people under investigation. Now, with his little disappearing act involving those murder suspects, that's our leverage right there. We have to turn him, and the only way to do that is to pin him all the way down. We have to find him and bring him down, then help him through the rest of the investigation..."

"What the fuck you mean, help him through the rest of the investigation?" barked Yella, confused to why would they bring him down then help him. It didn't make any sense.

"Once he gets pinned down with aiding and abetting charges helping murder suspects, he's going to need all the help in the world. Then that's when we come back in and save his ass, gaining his trust and loyalty."

"I'm not in. Ain't no way in hell I'm going to save a muthafucka who's trying to take my head off!" said Ken Cole.

"Your ass going to either help or go down by your muthafucking self. If it wasn't for those senseless murders you committed, then we wouldn't be in this fucking predicament in the first place!" replied Detective Grant at

Ken's comment, knowing he should be the last person not being a team player.

Ken just stood there, mouth twitching as he placed a black and mild cigar in his mouth and fired it up, taking a long pull, enjoying the sweet and smoothness of its flavor.

"Now, if I have all of your full attention, I have a plan, one that I'm quite sure if we execute well will fair in our favor. Right now none of us have any fucking choice." said Detective Grant.

"So, how do we get a hold of Fulwiley? Didn't the Captain say the feds had him?" asked Links, trying to figure out the impossible.

"Nah, they don't have him in custody yet. He's hiding somewhere, and the Captain is in on this as well. Her and Fulwiley is lovers, so it's natural she'd want to save her little bed mate. But we're going to set a trap so vicious that no one will be able to save his ass."

"I follow you with everything that you're saying, except one thing! How in the fuck is we going to set a trap for somebody when we don't even know where the fuck they're at?" asked Shandel as he leaned on the hood of his Lexus.

"Come on y'all, let me find out if you muthafuckas on drugs or something!" said Detective Grant as he looked at his crew from side to side, shaking his head in disappointment before he started talking. "We're the fucking police, we have access to any records the government has, as well as all the equipment to track every and anybody down...alive. Now, do y'all follow me?"

"Hell yea, I'm with you. Let's GPS his ass!" barked

Yella, knowing that was going to be his job anyways because he had all the hook ups at the station, especially in the Global Positioning Department. He was fucking the bitch Big Brina and they were seeing each other kind of seriously so it should be a piece of cake to get her to locate Officer Fulwiley without getting a tracking warrant, something they all knew they would never get.

"Yella, you're up next?" said Detective Grant.

"I'm already on it like yesterday!" replied Yella as he called Brina on the phone. He walked off and spilled his pitch at her giving her all the necessary information she needed to handle her business.

"Alright y'all, we're good. As soon as she locks a stable position in on him, she's going to give me a call."

"So, how long is this going to take?" asked Ken Cole, acting all paranoid because it wasn't no way in hell he was going to jail or prison for anything. He'd take anybody to war first.

"Nigga chill. Damn, you 'bout to stress me the fuck out with all these questions. It won't be five minutes, so just chill and let me do my magic." said Yella.

"Whatever man! Y'all nigga can chill but ain't no way in hell I'm going to even think about chilling as long as this investigation is going on. So, let's do what we have to do and get the fuck back to normal!" exclaimed Ken.

"I know right now everybody's mind is probably racing back and forth as well. As soon as we..."

Yella's phone interrupted Detective Grant as he was trying to comfort his squads comfort level.

"Yea, what's up Brina?" asked Yella, hoping she had

done located Fulwiley.

"I got him baby!"

"Where is he at?"

"Right now it shows him in Tampa at a residential address where he's been at for the past two hours.

"Tampa! Are you serious, Brina?"

"Positive. The address is..." and Yella cut her off.

"Come on baby, you know the drill. Text me the address okay?!"

"Alright, but you better bring your ass through tonight. I got this new Victoria's Secret lingere that I'm dying to wear for you!"

"I'll be there!"

"You better, and don't stand me up like you did the last time or I'm gon' fuck you up." said Big Brina, warning Yella, which he took good heed to. He knew Big Brina loved that abusive shit and he couldn't stand to have her make a scene on him.

"BINGO!" said Yella out loud after he hung up the phone with Brina.

"What's up, you got that info already?" knowing that had to be the reason he interrupted his flow.

"You damn skippy I do! It should be coming thru' the phone in a second." said Yella.

"Fuck all that! Where the fuck this muthafucka at?" barked Ken Cole.

"He ain't in Polk County, that's for sure!" stated Yella.

"What the fuck do you mean; he's not in Polk County? What, they got this muthafucka out of the country or something?" asked Ken, looking at Detective Grant like it was something he wasn't telling them.

"What the fuck you looking at me for? I have the slightest idea where he's at. If I did, I would have been went and snatched him up."

Yella waited until they were thru' with the back and forth bickering before he enlightened his crew.

"Y'all chill the fuck out! Our guy isn't out of the country or the state!" clarified Yella, "He's in Tampa, and has been at this particular residence for over two hours. I have no ideal whose residence, but I believe if we make a move right now we'll catch him before he gets missing." expressed Yella.

"You said Tampa, right?" inquired Shandel in his Jamaican accent.

"Yea!!!"

"We hit then, we can't fuck off in Tampa again. We got lucky last time when we snatched that informant up at the Hard Rock Casino."

"What informant?" asked Links, because this was one mission he didn't remember.

"You wasn't in on this. You was in Jamaica celebrating some Independence Festival!" said Detective Grant.

"Nah Dread, you wasn't with us when we snatched up John Boy."

"Aye, Aye, Aye!" screamed Detective Grant, pissed the fuck off at Ken for blurting out unnecessary information. Even though all of them was partners, what a nigga didn't already know, he didn't never need to know.

Everybody knew Ken had done fucked up, even Links as they shook their heads from side to side in disbelief.

Detective Grant feared for the worse with Ken. He knew with all of his heart that if they got squeezed, it came about because of Ken Cole. He talked entirely too much, and Detective Grant also knew it was time to start improvising just in case.

Yella's phone begin to chime, indicating to him he had a message. He instantly checked his message and it was Big Brina, on time as always. She had done sent the location as well as a satellite print out of the residence as well as Officer Fulwiley's car.

"Damn, this bitch good!" thought Yella as he shared the info with the rest of the squad. Detective Grant knew he was going to need his whole squad on this one. Tampa officials and Polk County officials did not get along, and what they were about to do was a criminal act, one that nobody but their selves needed to know about until they made it back to Polk County.

"Listen up fellas. Y'all already know what the deal is. Last time we got warned because of the badge, but you all know shit won't fly the same again. Right now I don't give a fuck, because if we don't grab this muthafucka up then we're fucked either way, so who's in with me?" asked Detective Grant, hoping everybody was down for this mission.

"Man you're trippin', what the fuck you mean; you hope everybody is down? Nigga we all in, you know the status!" barked Ken, because he wasn't about to go to jail or prison for anybody.

"Yea, count me in too. You know how we roll! Either together or never." said Yella.

"Yea mon', count us in Ras'clod!" stated Shandel as he gave his brother Links some dap.

"Alright, y'all gather around...here's the plan!"

Chapter 28

Back at the hospital everybody was in cheers. Especially Ms. Barbara Jean, as she stayed posted at her son's side. Devell had a successful recovery and the doctor said it would be no time before he was back able to fully function again. All Devell could think about was Tarrell, *"Where was she? Why wasn't she at his side? And, who did this to me?"* was the thoughts that overcrowded his mind.

Ms. Barbara Jean did her best trying to explain everything to her son, but all she knew was what happened at the Church. Lord knows she wished she had more to tell him, but she didn't. She did tell him about his friend that showed up, just knowing somebody cared enough to check on him made him light up with joy as he felt an inner strength spread throughout his weakened body. The doctors told him to relax as much as possible, and not to talk if he could help it, but Devell couldn't help it. He had to know who it was that came by to show him support.

"So momma, tell me who all came thru'?"

"Just the family, Tarrell, and the Church!"

"The Church, momma?" said Devell, like really.

"Yes baby, even Pastor Coward was here delivering the Holy Spirit. He prophesized that you would pull through just like you did."

"That's all good momma, but who else came thru'?" asked Devell, knowing it had to be more than just that. She talking 'bout my friends, but it seem like all those she name were her friends thought Devell.

"Oh, I'm sorry son, how could I forget!" said Ms. Barbara Jean before she was interrupted by her son.

"Forgot what momma?"

"That best friend of yours was here, him and that other boy you don't like. They said they'd be back, but nobody has shown up yet!"

"Momma, stop playing. You mean to tell me that King George is back in Polk County?!"

"Just as sure as me and you is talking!" she replied as she sat there beside the hospital bed and held her son's hand, all the while continuing to pray in her mind and thanking God for his recovery and a second chance at life. All Devell could do was lay back in the bed and stare at the life alert monitor that was plugged in to every vital point on his body just in case something went wrong and his body failed on him. The flat line machine would send a flat line beep all the way to the nurse's desk. He knew what and why King George was here for, *"Tarrell must've called him when she found out!"* he thought.

Devell wanted to be out there, right at his best friend's side as he wreaked havoc on everybody that had something to do with his current condition. A tear rolled down his eye, he didn't even try to wipe it away, he was in the company of his momma, the one person who knew that it wasn't any pussy in her baby boy. Devell felt his hand squeeze up, which gave him the indication that his momma noticed the tear. He kept his stare at the machine, away from his momma's, not even able to hear the visitor who just entered the room. Once Ms. Barbara Jean saw who it was that entered, her whole body lit up with excitement because she knew as long as they were together, they were going to protect one another. King George walked up to Ms. Barbara Jean who was like a mother to him and gave her a hug.

"How is he doing momma?" asked King George hoping she had some good news to tell him. Devell knew he wasn't losing his mind, he knew that voice from anywhere in the world. He turned around facing his momma and locked eyes with him, the only person he ever felt would die for him.

"Oh my God! I thought momma was pulling my leg when she said you was here. Nigga, you better come over here and give a nigga a hug bro." said Devell as ecstatic as he could possibly be.

"That's what's up!" responded King George as he leaned in and bear hugged his partner in crime for life, squishing him and the tubes that was attached to his body, making the machine malfunction, causing a flat line sound.

"Ohh Godd!!! Please tell me this ain't happening." pleaded Ms. Barbara Jean out loud.

The sound of the machine caught King George off guard, making him jump back off Devell, hoping he didn't apply too much pressure causing him any pain.

"Bro, you alright? Nigga say something!" demanded King George.

"Man, I'm good. You just put too much pressure on these tubes and it thought my circulation had cut off. I'll tell you what though, I'm ready to get the hell out of here."

"Boy, watch your mouth. You need to be thanking God instead of wasting your energy on cuss words!" said Ms. Barbara Jean, straightening her son out.

"Alright momma! I'll give God the praise!" said Devell all sarcastically.

"Help me up bro!"

"Son, the doctor said for you to get rest and not to be trying to move around."

"Momma, ain't no way I'm staying in this hospital bed another minute. Now is you going to help me or what?" asked Devell as he shifted his attention from his mother to his best friend.

"Bro you know I got you, but what are you trying to do, sit up or something?"

"Nigga, I'm trying to leave!"

"Oh Lord, please help this child of mines, for he don't know what he does!" confessed Ms. Barbara Jean.

"Bro, you just can't leave, we have to get a nurse or somebody to sign you out!"

"They better hurry up and sign me out or I'm going to be walking out. I have to get home and make sure my girl straight...she supposed to be right here with me so I can introduce y'all bro!"

"We already done that. Just chill for a second and let me go see if I can find somebody to get you up out of here the right way."

"Nah baby, you stay. I'll go and find somebody. I know y'all have so much to talk about!" said Ms. Barbara Jean.

"Okay momma, but hurry up because I'm dead serious about walking up out of here."

As soon as she left the room, they went straight to it.

"Bro, who did this to me?" asked Devell.

"I can't say, but I do know whoever shot you was riding shotgun with that nigga Damion Grey."

"I remember that part, but who and why? I just had dropped Damion off a few hours earlier and homie broke me off a few of them whole ones."

"Word!"

"Yea, that's on my dead baby's head."

"I got that nigga whereabouts too, and I'm going to run down on him something special as soon as I get you straight."

"Nigga you got me fucked up, I'm going to be the one who pull the trigger when Damion meet his maker."

"Bro you ain't in no condition to do anything. Just get back right so I can take you back to New York with me. You think you're ready for the show?" jokingly asked King George.

"Man, I been ready to come up there and put my gangsta down for the longest." exclaimed Devell as he waited on his partner to amp him up the way they always did one another all of their lives.

"Bro, that ain't what it is up there. Niggas ain't running around wilding in the streets like they do down here. That New York shit is on a whole different level, everything corporate thuggin'."

"Man, I ain't with that corporate shit, you already know my motto!" said Devell, letting his main man know that he wasn't about to let anybody put restraints on him or his gangsta.

"I know it sounds crazy and all with the corporate shit, but trust me bro. Shit goes from zero to one hundred real fast, just on a different level. I got you, I'll show you the ropes so everything will be a much easier transition than what it was for me and Big-O when we touched down up there."

"Why the fuck you bring that bitch ass nigga down here with you?" said Devell as thoughts of killing his untrustworthy ass flooded his mind.

"Bro, you trippin' right now. I know you wanna fuck him up because of taking your shit, but you have to let that shit go bro. You can't keep wearing that shit on your shoulders."

"Yea, that's easy to say when it's not your shit that he took. You wouldn't have even played with him and you know that!"

"You're wrong bro. As a matter of fact, I just sent that nigga on his way. Too much cruddy shit with him. But, I'm not gon' kill him because to me he's still family, but family I'm not fucking with!"

"Boy, that nigga had to do something real cruddy to have you turn your back on him. I never thought in a million years that I'd see this day!" stated Devell in a reasoning manner, hoping his main man spilled the beans to why he fell out with Big-O, but knowing King George the way he did, he knew that would never happen. They shared war stories for the next thirty minutes until Ms. Barbara Jean showed back up with the lead nurse in charge. She had to run a series of tests before she could discharge him from their care. After everything was said and done, and Devell had signed all of the medical waivers they needed, he was released to his own regard.

"Alright you two, I'm going to leave you because I know y'all have a lot of catching up to do. Just be careful, I don't know what I'd do if something was to happen to any one of you!" said Ms. Barbara Jean as she continued, "Come here and give me a hug, because ain't no telling when I'll see you rascals again!"

"Momma you're trippin', I'll never let you worry about me if I can help it!" responded Devell to his momma's concern, hoping to ease her worries a little.

"Yea momma, you know we're two the hard way!" added King George mimicking the name that the adults had given them when they was little kids, bringing all three of them to laughter.

"Call me son!"

"Will do momma!"

And before Ms. Barbara Jean made it out the door she informed him, "I got your car too, I'm going to park it in my garage until you're able to drive and maneuver around again."

"Alright momma, and thanks!" said Devell as he

watched his momma's head disappear on the other side of the door.

"Alright nigga, you're ready to get the fuck up out of here?"

"Hell yea, nigga wheel that wheelchair over here, I ain't trying to do no walking or standing up. You heard what that nurse said, or is you too gangsta to chaperone a real nigga?" asked Devell trying to put his seriousness on.

"Muthafucka get in this wheelchair before I drag your ass out of here. Coming at me with that flaw ass shit. When is you going to stop trying to use that fake ass psychology shit on a nigga? That shit for them hoe ass niggas, so keep it there!" warned King George, letting his main man know we ain't finna even play them ghetto games. All Devell was able to do was look up at his partner as he slid out of the bed into the wheelchair.

"Bro, I'm starving. Take me to get something to eat!" said Devell slumping down in the wheelchair as if he was in a low rider.

King George just shook his head at his best friends request as he got behind him and wheeled him up out of there to the all-black Humvee.

"Nigga, I know you on some treacherous shit because you don't even bring this muthafucka out unless you're tracking a bitch down!" said Devell.

"You damn right. And I'm not going to stop until I burn that fuck nigga alive who was responsible bro!"

"So you got a lead on them fuck niggas?"

"Nigga, what you think? You know I don't fuck off!"

"Well, let's go because I'm gon' kill that fuck nigga

who shot me, and his whole family." stated Devell angrily as he begin to lose his cool.

"Bro, you're trippin' nigga!"

"What the fuck you mean I'm trippin'?"

"Because the nigga that shot you, you already killed him!"

"How in the fuck I killed him, stop playing with me nigga. What, you think I'm slow or something. How in the fuck I kill somebody and I'm laid up in a muthafuckin' hospital?" yelled Devell at his big homie.

"Damn bro, you don't even remember what happened?!"

"Ain't a muthafuckin' thing happened if a bitch think they gon' pin a murder on me that I didn't commit."

"Come on nigga, get in and let me fill you in on what happened." said King George, helping Devell into the Humvee then placing the wheelchair in the back before getting in.

"Now tell me what the fuck happened!"

"Your momma said y'all was coming out of Church and this black car was approaching. She said you headed towards the car like you knew who it was and about the time the car made it close enough, the passenger window came down with a man leaning out shooting you. Your momma said every time she heard his gun bust a shot a part of her just left her body. She thought she had done lost you."

"Alright, alright. I get all of that. Tell me how the fuck I end up killing somebody."

"Your momma said on your way to the ground you

upped fire and shot back, blowing the gunman back through the window with half a face and half a chest. They found him on the next street over."

"Oh yea! I put that work in like that?" asked Devell all excitedly, not really remembering what the fuck went down but was gon' accept what he was hearing.

"Nigga you put that work in for real, Ms. Barbara Jean said the whole Church was out there. You had Jesus with you for real on this one because that nigga hit you up pretty good bro."

"I still can't believe Damion would even try my gangsta like this!" said Devell, knowing Damion was a dead man walking.

"They got his tag number and I ran it through, it came back to him so whether you fuck with the nigga or not he tried to get at you, and for that I'm going to put a bullet in his head."

All Devell could do was sit back in the large Captain seat the Humvee possessed as he thought heavily about, "Why Damion would even try to run down on him!"

"What's up bro, you're good?" asked King George as he sat there in the driver's seat looking at his main man as he displayed a look of discernment on his face. Not wanting to interrupt him much, he just allowed Devell to soak in whatever it was that had him far out there at the moment.

King George cut the massive machine on, the Humvee's air conditioning came to life. He turned up the stereo just a bit to let the sounds serenade while Trey Songz new hit song "Top Of The World" played while they headed out of the parking lot to Devell's house.

Chapter 29

The Police Force, the Sheriff's Office, Federal ATF Special Explosives Unit, as well as the FBI Bomb Squad was on site, they had St. Paul Projects roped off. You couldn't come in or out, everybody who lived in the proximity of the explosion was a potential suspect and authorities was treating everybody they questioned and encountered such as. A terrorist attack has been ruled out, so far there has been zero casualties which is extremely good for a blast of this magnitude. Luckily, one of the residents who occupied the apartment was the only one home and had just stepped out to visit the neighbor who lived directly across the hall when the blast occurred. As the explosion blew her completely off her feet through her neighbor's doorway for about twenty yards inside the house, slamming her frame up against the kitchen wall. She was knocked unconscious until her neighbor, Ms. Kat dashed her with a bucket of cold water, causing her to come to, but almost sending her into shock as the cold water made her hyperventilate like she was about to die.

Ms. Kat had called 911 only moments earlier because of the allegations that her neighbor had confessed to her stating she had been raped. But the explosion had Asia terrified and she wasn't uttering another word as she thought, *"If I would've just stayed inside the house like he said, none of this would have happened!"* Now she felt her life was about to be taken. Ms. Kat cooperated with the authorities as much as she could, but Asia wasn't fucking with them PERIOD. She was scared so she just sat balled up in the back of the ambulance as they treated her wounded body and the gash on her right cheek bone that sat high up almost to her eye.

Someone must have called Asia's momma because she came full force busting through the barricade straight to the back where the thick smoke from the explosion still hung low over St Paul in the night's air.

"Where my baby at? Please Lord don't let nothing be done happened to my precious baby!" pleaded Dot as she imagined life without her only child. Yea, they had their ups and downs, but Dot wouldn't trade in being her mother under no circumstances. Asia was her very own flesh and blood, and the only family she had left, except a brother of hers who lived in New York that she hasn't spoken to in almost seventeen years. Every since Asia was born when he tried to get Asia to live with him and his wife, and away from her mother's bad crack habit.

Dot had refused the offer and denied any contact from him since. She didn't need nobody's input in raising and taking care of her precious Asia. As she made it to the back, she saw where her apartment was smoldered in ashes, every single item she possessed was destroyed. Half of the apartment was blown away, making the lot that once housed her and her daughter looked like a toasted potato.

Asia heard her mother's cries as she leaped out of the back of the ambulance and dashed to her loving arms. "Momma! Here I go momma!" screamed back Asia as she leaped into her mother's arms, squeezing her so tightly you'd think she was under attack.

"Baby, thank God you're okay! What happened to our apartment?" she asked her daughter, but added before Asia could speak, "Don't even worry, you're all that matters. We could always find somewhere else to live." said Dot as she held Asia in her loving embrace.

"Momma, I'm so sorry for being disrespectful and for always fighting and arguing with you...I promise, I'll never disobey you again!" pleaded Asia as she cried uncontrollably.

"Baby, it's okay. Momma is going to protect you, even if it cost me my life doing so." said Dot as she turned all of her anger and hatred towards Damion. "He tried to take my precious baby from me!" she thought, knowing he meant trouble the first time she caught him trying to sneak into their house. Something about him ran chills through her body. But now she had revenge all over her, and she had intentions on carrying them out or fail trying. But first things first, she had to make sure her baby was safe. She had to do something she promised herself she would never do. She had to call him tonight.

"Let me look at you baby!" said Dot as she stepped

back to analyze her daughter's injury. Dot undid the bandage that was on Asia's face and saw the deep gash that altered her baby's look.

"Oh my God, what have he done to you."

Asia was speechless. *"How did my momma know what happened to me? Did she know my attacker? Did she send him to scare me?"* was all running through Asia's mind at the moment. Asia just had to ask.

"Momma, do you know what happened?" hoping her mother said the right thing. Because if she didn't it was about to be an all-out war right out here in the midst of everybody, fuck the police and all.

"Baby, I knew that boy didn't mean you no good from the start, it was just a matter of time before he tried to kill you. I've seen his kind for many years!" said Dot, trying to explain to her baby girl that she always feared for the worse with her and this old ass man who was old enough to be her damn daddy.

"Momma, what boy don't mean me no good?" asked Asia looking at her momma with her mouth pouted out.

"That damn Damion Grey. He just wasn't right for you but I stayed back and out of your way while you learned the hard way."

"Momma you're crazy! Come here and give me a hug."

Asia was happily relieved her momma had nothing to do with her attack. She felt guilty for even thinking her momma would send someone her way to harm her in the first place. It's just they have been beefing so hard lately, Asia wasn't about to put shit pass nobody, especially after she was almost killed tonight.

"Excuse me ma'am, we've been looking all over for you!" said the paramedic, "We have to get you to immediate surgery."

"What do you mean immediate surgery?" barked back Dot.

"Ma'am, is you a relative of any sort?" asked the short Asian looking man who looked like a terrorist than a fucking paramedic.

"Yes I am. I'm her mother and I want to know why my baby needs to have immediate surgery, because if it's not life threatening, then it ain't no way in hell she's being put to sleep!" demanded Dot as thoughts of her childhood came racing back to her mind. Her sister had fell out of a tree and had to get surgery. Unfortunately, she never recovered from the dosage of anesthesia she was given. Dot was lost to the world ever since, and blamed her drug addiction from the loss of her sister. But it wasn't no way in hell she was about to repeat that same encounter with death again.

"Ma'am, the explosive technicians have discovered a large amount of cyanide was used to make the bomb, so when it exploded the cyanide went airborne and spreaded like a fungus, so we'll have to remove the torn tissue and replace it with artificial skin samples to ensure she wasn't taminated."

"Remove what and replace what?" Said Asia all confused with the technical language the paramedic was using.

"Basically ma'am, we'll have to do reconstructive surgery to make sure that none of that cyanide entered your open wound, because if so, then you wouldn't have three more hours to live."

Dot went crazy when she heard that.

"Oh my God, Lord please take care of us at this very moment. Whatever my baby done to deserve this, let me suffer for it. She's only a child Lord and haven't even lived yet. I ask you Lord to protect her in the name of Jesus...Amen!" prayed Dot as her eyes welled up with tears.

"We're wasting time, ma'am. A special procedure has been ordered and we're already late. We have to go now!" ordered the paramedic.

"Momma, I'm scared. What's happening? Please don't let me die!"

"Baby, I'm not going to let nothing happen to you. I'll be right here by your side, okay?!"

"Okay momma."

"Could you please come with me young lady?" asked the paramedic as he gently placed his hand on the base of her elbow as he led Asia back to the ambulance with Ms. Dot in tow, right behind them. As soon as they made it inside the ambulance, they harnessed Asia into the stretcher, hooking her up to the I.V. tubes, sedating her, allowing her to fall into a deep sleep. They wanted her to be as calm as possible before surgery so she wouldn't enter into an induced coma. Dot feared the worse, all she could do was pray. She pulled out her phone and strolled through her contacts until she found what she was looking for.

Dot pressed the call button and called the one person whose voice she dreaded ever hearing again. To her, he was dead. But unfortunately, some situations call for drastic measures, and her daughter's life was one of those situations. The first ring seemed like it lasted an eternity. As Dot waited for someone to pick up, she got lost for a moment as she stared at her precious baby who laid motionless on the harness. She almost didn't hear the mad man on the other end as he begin to spit obscene gestures, thinking he had a prank caller on the line.

"Eddie, Eddie...stop cursing. It's me, your sister Dorothy!" said Dot trying to get her brother's attention, but he kept on raging through the phone.

"Be a man and show yourself, you muthafuckas always want to call somebody's damn phone and not say a fucking word. That's some rude ass shit and I hope your stank ass choke to death! Want to play on my muthafucking phone. I hope you know I got caller I.D. and when I find out who this is I'm personally going to hunt you down and stick my knife in you, just keep playing and think I'm something to play with!" barked Eddie through the phone, almost hanging up until he heard his name being screamed through the phone.

"EEDDIIEEE!!!" screamed out Dot.

"Who the fuck is this?" barked Eddie.

"This Dorothy, your sister!"

"Dorothy! Who...Oh shit!" he said, kind of excited, "What the fuck you calling me for after sixte..."

"It's been sixteen years, five months, and twenty-one days." recited Dorothy, cutting off her brother.

"Damn, you remember all that?"

"You damn right I do, that's when you tried to take my precious baby away from me!"

"I would never do that, it's just at the time you wasn't

fit to raise her right and as her uncle, I wanted to help make raising her right possible."

"I see you're still crazy as hell, thinking I wasn't fit to raise my own damn baby. You see I did it! And that was with no help at all!"

"Yea, I applaud you for that. But, if you wasn't so stubborn, the both of your lives would have been a whole lot better."

"Anyways, I ain't call you for no lectures or any apologies because I'm not trying to give any."

"Well, what in the hell did you call me for? We could have left things how they were because I was fine!"

"Whatever nigga. I have to send Asia up there with you for a while until things clear up down here!"

"Send who?" asked Eddie, forgetting his own niece's name.

"Asia, you jackass, your got-damn niece!" yelled Dot.

"Why now? What the hell have she done that you have to send her up here?"

"Some man she's dating is trying to kill her and I think it would be best if she had a change of scenery!"

"Hold on for a moment, I'm not trying to take somebody else's problems because if she gon' bring all that drama up here, she might as well keep her tail down there!"

"EDDIE I'M NOT ASKING YOU, I'M TELLING YOU!" xemanded Dot as a brief silence hovered over the phone.

"When is she coming?"

"Probably in about a week or so. I have to hustle up some money to send her up there. Plus, she's being rushed to the hospital right now, we're both in the ambulance."

"Y'all both are what? Dorothy, what the fuck is going on?" asked Eddie, because even though him and his sister didn't speak, he always loved her and not a single day that passed by he didn't pray for her.

"I'll explain all that later. Just get ready for your niece!"

"Hey sis, let me know when you're ready okay, I'll send the money. I told you I've always been here to help!" said Eddie as he added, "What does she looks like?"

Dot knew her answer was going to be too much for him to handle, having to look at Asia each and every day as she looked like her dead sister, damn near her identical twin.

"She looks like Precious!"

Hearing those words almost sent lumps in Eddie throat as he tried to clear it because he knew the best thing for him to do was leave that subject alone and deal with it when he came face to face with it.

"Well sis, call me when you're ready." and just like that their conversation was over, but a flood of emotions had just been opened as Eddie's childhood replayed itself over and over again as he blamed himself for not holding onto his sister up in that tree the day she fell and lost her life. Dot was relieved a little. She knew sending her daughter to live with Eddie was the best thing, but was Eddie ready for Asia? That was what bothered Dot more than anything as she sat back in the ambulance and allowed the sirens to play music to her ears.

Chapter 30

Old man Larry had done made it to Bartow. K-Boy had called one of his workers from their other trap house that sat across town on Polk Street. He was supposed to meet up with Old Man Larry and give him some guns. Old Man Larry pulled the white Ford Econo van into the Winn-Dixie parking lot off of Highway 60 and parked his van between the back side of K.F.C. and McDonalds and waited for the drop. After about fifteen minutes a tan colored bubble Caprice pulls up with limo tint, facing the opposite direction of Larry's van, making their driver's side face each other. The driver in the Caprice rolled his window down as well. Larry obliged, leaning just a nudge out of the window to get in hearing distance.

"What's happening folk?" asked Larry, knowing this had to be the mark he was supposed to meet. This nigga looked and fit the bill of some sort of gun dealer. He wore a Kuffi on top of his head and had a big droopy ass, bushy beard like he was from the Middle East. You could tell he was Muslim.

"That's the package on the back seat!" He said as he reached back there and unlocked the back door.

Old man Larry didn't wanna waste any more time than he had to, so he hurried down out of the van and opened up the rear driver side door revealing at least a six-foot-long canvas, army green duffle bag. Old Man Larry grabbed the bag, closed the door back, and hopped back into the van. Immediately he checked the contents. He may have been old and looked foolish, but he was far from anybody's fool. Old Man Larry knew how fucked up these young niggas were teaming up with the law, setting their own kind up. Rummaging through the bags contents, Old Man Larry was satisfied with what he had just received from K-Boy's soldier.

It was three Bushmaster ACR Assault rifles with folding stocks, six one hundred round clips, three military grade light weight bulletproof vests, and four identical Glock.40's. Old Man Larry knew his weapons, his fascination for guns is what led him to join the Armed Forces back in the 70's, when he got deployed to the Vietnam War. But throughout his life, he kept up with all the latest firearms, and Larry knew by the contents in the duffle bag that each and every weapon in there was the latest on the market. Larry closed the duffle back up and headed back to Tampa to the LaQuinta Inn, where Tenille, K-Boy, and Joann was patiently waiting.

"I hope these young cats ready to handle their issue!" thought Old Man Larry, because it wasn't no turning back. A lot of blood was about to be shed and lives lost. If they wasn't careful, their lives could be some of the ones lost. Old Man Larry took the time as he drove to reflect back on his life, both the good and the bad and he couldn't help but smile. Larry was satisfied with his brief life assessment. He'd lived his life to the fullest and now it was time to give back. He had to show his lil homies the way. It was cool to get all the money and have people admire you, but at the end of the day none of that shit mattered if nobody respected you. "I rather be feared than loved!" was the last thing on Larry's mind as he blended in with the traffic.

Chapter 31

Jumping out of his Dodge Charger, Officer Fulwiley hurriedly walked over to the driver's door of the Maserati with disgust drawn over his face. Chineir just sat there behind the wheel, her eyes hid behind the Dolce and Gabana shades as she stared straight ahead, afraid to look in the officer's direction.

"Tap, Tap, Tap!" was the sound as Officer Fulwiley knocked on the driver's window with his knuckles. Chineir slowly turned to face him, pressing the button for the window to roll down, stopping it three quarters of the way. Officer Fulwiley leaned over onto the car, resting his elbows on the roof top as he was able to see directly through the top part of the window.

"So, pretty lady! Tell me something. Where were you going in such a hurry?" asked Fulwiley as he began to lose control from the perfume aroma that escaped the car's confines, racing at speeds unknown through his nostrils all the way to his brain, causing him an instant hard on. He was caught up in the moment, never has he witnessed or been in the presence of a bad bitch like the one sitting in the car. He pictured himself pulling on her long ass pony tail while he fucked her from the back.

"Why are you back so soon?" responded Chineir as she shook violently with fear throughout the inside of her body.

"I came to get what's owe to me, or have you and your sister forgot about the deal that we made?"

Chineir wanted to tell the cop to go and fuck himself, but she knew that would be like digging her own grave. "What do you want? We don't have any money!"

"I think you know exactly what I want!"

That statement scared Chineir much more. She done fucked and sucked her share of niggas. Some ugly ass ones as well as some fine ass ones. But it was all from her free will. One thing a woman dreaded most was to be forced into having sex with somebody they didn't want to have sex with. Chineir knew she had to do something. She didn't want to provoke him the least bit. She was home alone and it wasn't no telling where Moneisha was or Odell.

"I'm sorry, but no. I do not know what you want!" said Chineir, trying to buy a little time hoping some miracle would transpire.

"I'll tell you what, why don't you unlock the door and take me inside."

"Take you inside for what? I'm fine right here!" Stated Chineir.

"Chineir! It's Chineir isn't it!"

Chineir nodded her head yeys.

"I'm trying not to become mad and disappointed. Do

you know what happens when I become mad and disappointed?"

"NOOOOO!!"

"Well, I'll tell you what happens. People end up hurt or in jail. Now, which one do you want to happen?" said Officer Fulwiley, putting stronger emphasis on the situation, playtime was over.

"I don't want you getting mad, just give me a moment sir!"

Chineir knew she had to do something. So she might as well get it over with and out of the way she thought as she found the right words to say.

"Okay, I'll play with you if that's what you want, but only under one condition..." demanded Chineir.

"And what condition is that?" asked Officer Fulwiley as he looked at this bitch as if she had lost her damn mind, "Who the fuck she think she is to call any shots? I should get the bitch arrested just for trying me!" he thought.

"Leave my family out of this and I'll do whatever you want, how you want it, and whenever you want it done!" offered Chineir hoping he accepted her offer because it would kill her knowing somebody hurt her twin sister.

"And why should I settle for you when I can have you and your sister?"

"Trust me, I'm more than enough for you! Once you had some of this, you would never want anything else!" said Chineir all assuredly. All she needed now was this cop to accept her offer and she was about to bring out the trick bag on his ass.

"Alright, I accept. But, I'm telling you right now that if

your shit ain't like that, then I'm applying the pressure not only on you and your sister, but also on that murdering cousin of yours!" said Fulwiley, trying to scare the bitch more than what she already was. Chineir didn't say another word. She pressed the window button and rolled it back up, then hit the unlock button as she opened the door and stepped out.

"Got-damn! This bitch super bad!" thought Officer Fulwiley. He knew she was tuff from the other night, but looking at her and how she damn near busted out of the black body suit she was rocking, had his manhood throbbing.

Chineir was able to look him in the eyes. She wasn't no small bitch, and with the Derion booties she was wearing it gave her already five foot eleven frame a slight advantage.

She grabbed the officer by his mid-section, gripping her hands around his belt buckle, pulling him behind her as she took off in seductive strides into the house, man handling the cop as if he was a weak little child. Not even realizing it, Chineir had left her car on in the garage, with the garage wide open. The only thing that was on her mind was to break this crooked ass cop off so he can get the fuck on his way. She walked the cop straight pass the foyer into the den and pushed him down onto the cream leather sofa.

"I want to get in your bed!" stated Fulwiley.

"Not yet, tuff guy. Make it thru' this and we'll work our way up to my bed!" said Chineir, teasing the shit out of the cop. Just the statement alone had him overly excited. He begin to imagine the positions he would fuck her in.

"I'm going to try and bust one inside this bitch!" he

thought as he laid back on the sofa, making himself comfortable.

"Take your muthafuckin' clothes off!" she demanded.

Officer Fulwiley didn't even hesitate to follow her orders. He was butt ass naked. He was out of everything but his socks. He wasn't about to expose his bunions to her just yet. His feet was something awful, and he had to get to know her before he took it that far.

Chineir wasn't tripping about any of that. She done fucked plenty of niggas who kept their socks on. She knew they were ashamed of their feet. She pushed Fulwiley back into the couch and seductively got naked as well. Starting with taking off her shades, then kicking off the Derion booties. Seeing her perfectly pedicure toes, Officer Fulwiley mouth got watery. He wanted to put her whole foot in his mouth. Seeing that she had his full attention, she peeled the one-piece cat suit off her body, revealing her full nakedness. She didn't have on a bra or panties and she was clean shaven. Chineir knew she had his attention, but after seeing her perfectly shaped body, she had stole more than his attention. She noticed his already erect penis standing straight out at attention. What she had in mind, Chineir knew he wasn't ready for it.

She crawled onto the couch beside him and turned upside down. Officer Fulwiley looked at her like she had lost her damn mind, until she crawled onto him resting her arms and elbows onto his thighs, leaving her legs spreaded wide open, balancing herself with her knees as they rested on his shoulder blades. All Officer Fulwiley was able to see was pussy. The way she had her legs open automatically opened up her pussy lips, revealing her pretty pink insides. Her asshole was on display as well. It almost looked like a pussy itself the way it's hole opened up. Officer Fulwiley couldn't take it no more. He gripped her ass cheeks and pulled her into his mouth.

"UMMMM UMMMM!!" was all Fulwiley could say after he tasted her sweetness. He could spend the rest of his life just like this he thought. Her ass was so soft, each cheek felt like it was going to melt in his hands.

Officer Fulwiley wasn't no rookie when it came to a woman's sexual pleasures. he felt he could give the best a run for their money, which is what He was about to do right now. He took the tip of his tongue and tickled the outer surface of Chineir's pussy, flicking it back and forth over her clitoris. He had her juices boiling. She was so wet, Fulwiley's whole face and mouth was soaked in pussy juice. It was time for her to join the party. She opened her mouth up all the way and stuck it over his dick, making all of him disappear in thin air. Once she had all of him in her mouth and throat, she clamped down with her lips, using the moistness of her mouth and tongue as she sucked his dick from the bottom all the way to the tip of its head, making a popping sound when she released it.

"Oh shitttt! Bitch, what the fuck is you doing down there?" asked Fulwiley damn near biting her clitoris clean off. Never before have he experienced a rush shoot through his dick like that before, and as much as he was enjoying burying his face between her legs and ass, Fulwiley wanted to see with his own eyes.

"Shut the fuck up and get to eating, I didn't say you

could talk!" ordered Chineir as she began to take control, bringing her legs in closer, locking his head in. She was about to fuck him all the way up. Fulwiley obeyed his command as he took his tongue and stuck it inside her asshole. She was so wet back there you'd think it was her pussy. Chineir was loving the feeling, she was super crazy about anal sex and this nigga done sparked her fuse and he didn't even know it.

Chineir dropped her mouth back over his dick, repeating her lollipop trick until she adjusted her jaws to his medium size dick. It didn't take long before she had his toes curled up, he never had a mouth wrapped around his dick like this before. He was in la-la land, and wasn't trying to come back.

Chineir started using her ass muscles making each butt cheek vibrate, one of her many tricks she learned at her job when she needed one of them thirsty ass, hungry niggas to empty their pockets. She wasn't trying to hit his police ass off for any money. She was on a mission to fuck his mind up. She wanted him on her own little yo-yo string. "This muthafucka think shit sweet! When I'm thru' with his ass, he'll be completely under my spell." thought Chineir as she continued to suck his dick, working her tongue against his pee hole like she was trying to enter it. Chineir felt his dick begin to throb, she knew that sign from anywhere. This nigga was about to cum and she wasn't about to let up on his ass. She went to deep throating him, sucking his dick like she was riding it. His legs went from wide open to closed, she had his knees knocking. Fulwiley couldn't hold it back any longer. He let his eyes roll back in his head and exploded one of the biggest loads ever. He waited for her to throw a fit but she didn't. She swallowed every drop of him until his dick had turned into a miniature weenie. When Chineir released the clamp she had on Fulwiley's head, rolling off of him, she was surprised at how wet his face was, all gooey and shit. She had done sneaked an orgasm in and didn't even know it. She was an animal, it didn't take much for her to nut. You could run a finger across her pussy and she would get to leaking. She was just that high natured.

Chineir sat up beside Officer Fulwiley with his limp dick in her hands. She started jacking it, building back up an erection because she wanted to be fucked and even though it wasn't a huge dick Fulwiley had, it would have to do for now. Looking at him, Chineir saw that he wasn't a bad looking man. He was actually cute and if he played fair, she didn't mind fucking with him from time to time.

When she got him back rock hard, she mounted on the couch in doggy style position, with her ass hanging out and her face buried in the back of the couch. She didn't have to tell Fulwiley what she wanted him to do, he jumped up immediately and rubbed his dick across her pussy lips until he found the opening he was looking for then plunged his dick inside of her hot wet love box.

"Oh my Gosh! I can stay inside of you forever!" confessed Fulwiley to the sensation of her pussy.

Chineir had to turn around because she wanted to see the look on his face. It always turned her on seeing how helpless a man became when they was deep in some good pussy. What Chineir saw, she wasn't looking for as she saw her cousin come up from behind the cop as he tried to get his groove on. Her face went from enjoyment to concernment.

"Break yourself fuck boy!" demanded Odell, as he held the barrel of his .40 cal onto the back of Officer Fulwiley's head, literally scaring the shit out of him, making him stink up the room which pissed Odell all the way off. Odell popped him upside the head by his temple knocking his ass slap out.

"Cuz, why did you hit him? You probably killed him!" said Chineir, now more scared than what she was. Looking at the blood ooze from the police's head, Chineir thought he was dead for real.

"Fuck that pig, cuz. Moe called me and told me what's up so I hurried up over here before that nasty cop hurt you."

She wasn't about to tell Odell that this was all her idea. Hell naw, she was going to play the victim role all the way to the end.

Chineir started crying and jumped into her cousin's arms. She knew Odell would always protect them.

"Come on Chi-Chi, help me tie this muthafucka up!"

"Tie him up for what cuz? What are you going to do to him?" she asked hoping with everything inside of her that he didn't say he was going to kill him.

"I don't know yet cuz, but for starters we have to tie him up. Go and grab that fishing line out of the garage."

"Okay, but let me call Moe first and let her know that I'm okay." she said reaching for her phone off the end table.

"Don't worry about that, I'll call her. You just run and grab that fishing line like I told you!"

Chineir took off for the garage while Odell called Moneisha. She picked up on the first ring as if she was already anticipating the call.

"Hello, Hello!" answered Moneisha.

"What's up cuz, this Odell!"

"Where are you? Did you make it to the house?" asked Moe frantically.

"Yea, I'm at the house right now and Chi-Chi is okay. Good thing I made it here on time because this crooked ass police looked like he was gon' try to fuck Chi-Chi over."

"Thanks Odell, I love you so...." and before Moneisha could get out her next words, all you heard was "BOOOOM!" as the deafening sound demanded his immediate attention as he abruptly turned its way. What he witnessed next almost made his heart stop beating as Chineir's body came sliding towards him in a frontwards dive. As soon as she hit the floor, Odell dropped the phone from his ear and went to dumping, shooting straight chest shots. It was no use. All five of the masked intruders had on bullet proof vests. When Odell realized all that, he was out of bullets.

"ODELL!" screamed Moneisha through the phone, but nobody answered. She instantly knew that shit had turned for the worse.

"Take me home, now!" demanded Moe as she looked over at Bimp, letting the tears flow effortlessly down her cheeks.

"Baby what's up? You good?" asked Bimp, kinda glad because now he could skip taking her to get something to eat and get straight to meeting up with the plug.

"No, I'm not good! Just get me home...please!!" screamed Moneisha.

"Baby, if something is wrong, tell me. I can help you, but you have to let me help you!"

Moneisha went to getting hysterical, pounding on his dash board as she slammed her body back and forth against the seat. Bimp weaved the Jaguar SUV off the highway onto the right emergency bank and got control of the situation because lil momma was trippin' and he didn't want her to think that he didn't care about her.

"Listen! Whatever it is you're going thru', whatever it is that's bothering you, I want it to bother me as well. You know I have this meeting with the plug to pick up a major package, but I'm about to cancel that because I'm not leaving your side. Moneisha, I love you baby. I know you may have a rocky past, but that's your past. I'm your future. So from here on out, if you let me, I want to protect you, and I mean that whether it cost me my own life!" pleaded Bimp, hoping Moneisha would fall for his smooth lover boy game and tell him that everything is fine, she's just having a moment. But if Bimp was waiting on that, then he'll be waiting a long time. What Moe heard through the phone, she couldn't help but fear for the worse.

"I think somebody just shot my cousin!"

"Somebody did what?"

"I was on the phone with my cousin Odell, and I heard a loud boom, then the phone went blank."

"Are you sure it was a gunshot you heard?" asked Bimp, "Because a lot of sounds could imitate a gunshot sound."

"I know what a gunshot sounds like!" said Moneisha sternly.

"Was anybody else with him?" asked Bimp, hoping to bring some logic to the situation.

"Yea, my twin!"

"Did you try calling her?"

"No, but...."

"But what? Call her, because I'm quite sure they're both alright." said Bimp, trying to comfort her, but none of that shit was working as the phone kept on ringing.

"Ohhhh God, please don't let nothing bad happen to my family!" pleaded Moneisha, "Nobody's picking up!" she screamed.

"Alright baby, were nothing but a few blocks away. You said you heard a gunshot, right? Well then, let's go handle this beef." said Bimp as he jumped back onto the highway, catching the next exit that led to their house. They were there in no time. Moe noticed the unfamiliar vehicles in the yard. She didn't recognize not one of them other than Odell's SUV.

"Who all cars is those?" asked Bimp.

"I don't know!" replied Moneisha all dumbfounded.

"Alright, how many ways are there in and out of there?" asked Bimp as he parked in the next door neighbor's yard and flipped the back seat up, unveiling the hidden compartment that he kept his artillery in. He grabbed the AR-15 Carbine, two extra fifty round clips, and a High Point bullet proof vest. He handed Moneisha a Glock .9mm with the extended clip, holding thirty rounds each and told her all she had to do was aim and pull the trigger. The gun will do the rest.

"It's the pool patio, the garage, the side entrance, and the front door."

"Alright, I'm coming thru' the back pool area. I want you to catch anybody who come running out. Don't let nobody get pass you!" ordered Bimp as he jumped out of his SUV and trotted along the side of the house to the back. As soon as he reached the pool patio, he peeked through the sliding glass door and saw all of the ruckus that was transpiring. He saw it was five of them, all of them wearing masks...it was now six of them. One of them came walking up with a rag held onto the side of his head as if he was injured. Bimp scanned the room for his bitch's twin and their cousin. But what he saw made him drop his head. He instantly knew the body on the floor was Chineir's, and the one hanging from the ceiling had to be Odell's.

"Damn!" was all Bimp could say because he knew shit was going to to be fucked up just trying to hold lil momma down. "Oh well, here goes nothing!" he thought as he quietly slid through the door and braced himself behind the island top that separated the kitchen from the foyer. Nobody had an ideal what was next as Bimp took aim at the two masked men that was standing together and pulled the trigger to his AR-! 15 letting out a burst of rounds, dropping them both.

Instantly, the other masked men went to shooting back but their automatic handguns were no match to the fully automatic assault rifle that Bimp was using.

"Four down, two more to go!" thought Bimp as he came out into the opening in a standoff with the one who had the towel up to his head. He looked to be holding a forty-five. Bimp laughed at the notion and squeezed the trigger on his rifle, tearing his target's shoulder off before the chamber went blank.

"Shit!" screamed Bimp, knowing these few seconds it was going to take to reload could mean life or death. His assailant had to know exactly what he was thinking because the last masked man jumped out with a double barrel shotgun and went to blasting. Bimp dived back behind the island counter in just a nic of time as he inserted the fully loaded clip inside the AR and came back up gunning like he was part of the ISIS terrorist group. The masked man tried to flee for cover, but it was too late. Bimp caught him in the back of his hind leg making him stumble as he tried to flee back through the garage. Bimp came racing up from behind him and looked down at the one who he just blown his shoulder off and aimed the assault rifle at his face.

"WAIT!!!" screamed the injured man as he held his good arm up as if he was going to stop the slug from entering his body. "I'm a fucking cop, we're all cops!" said Officer Fulwiley, hoping the cop statement would bring some sense into this mad gunman. But it was no use, Bimp squeezed the trigger letting off two close range rounds, blasting part of his held out hand off as the bullets made its way to his chest and face, killing him instantly.

Bimp looked up at Odell hanging from the tier and felt sympathy for his soul, but had to keep it moving as he chased behind the other masked man through the garage.

"SKUURRRD!!"...."VRRRRMMM!!" was the sound from the smoke grey Dodge Charger as it fish tailed up out of there.

"Damn!" Bimp said as he lowered his aim, unable to take a clean shot with the assault rifle. He knew shooting out in the open like this would bring problems he didn't have time for. He already had to answer for the murders inside the house.

"Oh shit!" he thought as he looked around for Moneisha. Bimp raced over to his SUV and looked inside, but no Moneisha. "Where the fuck is this bitch at?" Bimp looked around and saw this middle aged white woman coming across the lawn from next door.

"Hello Sonny! Excuse me!" said the woman, stealing Bimp's attention as he caught a clear look at her figure.

"Damn, this bitch bad." he thought as he noticed the full-figured breast standing at attention, small waist and hips poking out through the skin-tight sweats, looking like she was in the middle of a work out session. Bimp lowered the rifle to his side as he paid attention to what the woman had to say.

"You're looking for the pretty lady that stays here?" asked Ms. Betty.

"Yea! You seen her? Where did she go?" asked Bimp, hoping that the old lady knew.

"That guy in the car that sped off took her with him!"

"What you mean, took her with him?" asked Bimp, knowing this couldn't be happening.

"He put her in his trunk and took off!" she said, sighing after her statement.

"Damn...Damn, Damn, Damn!" grunted Bimp as he

slammed the stock of the AR-15 into the driveway repeatedly from the frustration he was experiencing at the moment.

"This might help you sir!" said the middle-aged woman as she held out a piece of paper.

"What it this?" asked Bimp as he took the paper from her.

"It's his tag number..."

Chapter 32

Joann was driving the white Ford Econoline as she slowly crept up the street in the residential neighborhood that one of Tenille and K-Boy's goons had given them the address to, which supposed to have been Devell's crib. They didn't see the burgundy Lincoln nowhere in sight as Old Man Larry, K-Boy, and Tenille peeped out the tinted windows of the van. Tenille wasn't fooled at all, he noticed the house had a two-car garage and figured Devell must keep that car in the garage.

"Baby, hit the block one more time and let me see something!" said Old Man Larry, trying to figure out each and every scenario just in case shit went sour.

Joann did as she was told, she had one of the Glock .40's in her lap from the stash of guns Larry had picked up earlier. Joann knew her shit, and she wasn't afraid to pull the trigger if she had to. Right now, she was ready to ride or die with her man. Her loyalty to him reached beyond measure. After they looped the block for the third time,

Joann was back on Devell's street, creeping, slowly approaching the middle where his house sat.

"Hold up baby! Watch that Humvee coming up!" warned Old Man Larry as he put Joann up on the approaching vehicle coming up the opposite side of the road, looking like some sort of military style equipment.

"Baby, what you want me to do? Just keep going?" asked Joann.

"Yea, hit the block one more time. We have to do this shit right because I'm trying to keep us all out of jail and out of the grave yard." stated Larry as he paid attention to the all-black Humvee in front of him, hoping to get a look at its occupants inside. He didn't even notice the big ass nigga exit the house as Big-O walked up to his Maybach Benz and grabbed something out of the trunk.

K-Boy wasn't wasting another second. All he could think about was how this nigga just tried to murk him and his fam. Tenille read K-Boy's mind and cocked the chamber back on the bushmaster he had fumbling around in his hands. K-Boy followed suit as well. The van was moving on the same side of the street where Devell's house sat, as soon as Joann made it dead center, Tenille and K-Boy jumped out.

"Dammit!" was all Old Man Larry could say as he jumped out as well with two of the Glock .40's cocked back and aimed at the big nigga, not knowing what was up because his lil homies ain't bust one shot yet.

"Fuck nigga, tighten up!" screamed out K-Boy as Tenille and Old Man Larry kind of circled him.

"Nigga, where the fuck that pussy ass nigga Devell

at?" continued K-Boy, demanding answers.

"Nigga fuck you and fuck that nigga!" barked back Big-O, "Y'all bitch ass niggas might as well do what y'all came to do because I'm not a rat and I don't got a fuck thang for ya!"

The revved up engine stole everybody's attention as the black Humvee jumped the lawn and came racing full speed at them. Big-O knew exactly who it was behind the wheel, which gave him enough time to try and make a run for the house where his gun was sitting on top of the table right next to the door's entrance.

Everybody tried to take cover and get out of harm's way. Tenille went left while K-Boy went right. Old Man Larry held his ground and stayed focused on what he came here for, the nigga Devell. He wasn't about to let him make it inside of the house, they only had one shot at it and he was taking it.

Larry aimed the Glock .40 at his target and went to unloading bullet after bullet. Big-O was only five feet away from the door when the first bullet struck him. He kept on pacing until the second bullet hit him in the middle of his back, striking his vertebrae, paralyzing him in midair. Four more rounds caught Big-O before he hit the ground. Tarrell ran outside just as Big-O fell face first at her feet.

"NOOOOOO!!!!" she screamed, "Not my baby, please God don't let him die!" she pleaded as she dropped down to her knees and rolled Big-O's body over, trying to resuscitate him back to life, but it was no use, Big-O was headed to meet his maker.

King George couldn't believe what he was witnessing,

his muthafuckin' childhood friend had just got gunned down right in his muthafuckin' face. He mashed the pedal a little harder, accelerating the massive Humvee, slamming its front grill through the back of the gunman, pinning him to the front bumper as he smashed him in between the Humvee and Big-O's new Mercedes Benz causing an impact so forceful, one of the gunman's eyes popped out of his head as brain matter followed, leaking out of his eye socket.

Tenille and K-Boy couldn't believe what had just happened to Old Man Larry. They didn't understand why Larry gunned the big man down, he wasn't their target. They both tried to race back to the van but it was no use. When Joann saw the love of her life go down, all she wanted to do was get the fuck out of there. She took off in the van, haul tailing the fuck back to Bartow. K-Boy and Tenille was devastated at the moment. They both stood in the middle of the road with the Bushmaster assault rifles in their hand. Unable to run much because of their injuries. They both turned back towards the action. "Might as well handle what they came here for!" they thought, but somehow they knew it was useless.

The bullet from King George's pistol seemed to take forever as it traveled through mid-air. Tenille saw it coming, he couldn't even blink because in just the little time it took to do so, the bullet had already caught him in the center of his eyes, knocking him off his feet onto his back in the middle of the road. K-Boy lost it, he went to squeezing the trigger to the bushmaster sending rounds flying everywhere. King George wasn't even trying to play with that assault rifle. He knew the damage that bitch would do.

All Devell could do was sit in the Humvee shocked. What he was witnessing in front of his very own eyes had him burning with fire beyond his control. When Big-O went down, his fiancé jumped to his aid like she was his bitch. And here he was in a hospital fighting for his life. One of K-Boy's stray bullets struck Tarrell in her stomach, sending her tumbling over. All she could do was clutch her wound, hoping it wasn't as bad as it felt. Unfortunately, K-Boy had run out of bullets and all the other clips was inside of the van with Joann. K-Boy knew his time had done come as well, but he wasn't about to give up. If the nigga Devell wanted him, he had to work a little harder.

K-Boy reached down for Tenille's rifle, but on his way up, before he could swing the fully automatic weapon into use, King George sent a burst of rounds his way, catching K-Boy in the neck, mouth, forehead, his neck again, and his arm finishing off the last of the trio that showed up at his main man's crib. Devell got out of the Humvee, barely able to move. He didn't even attempt to use the wheel chair that was in the back of the vehicle. Devell stumbled all the way over to where the one guy stood dead, smashed between the Humvee and Mercedes and picked up the handgun that he'd dropped. King George just stood there, looking, hoping his main man ain't waste no extra energy because he had done took care of all the fake ass gangstas who came and tried to bust a move. But what Devell had in his mind King George couldn't possibly fathom. The way he was dragging his body, Devell was moving like a snail as he made it to Big-

O's already dead body and pumped three rounds into his face.

"I told you what I'd do if I ever saw you again. I made you a promise that I would shoot you in your face. Well, I keep my promises!" said Devell as he talked to the dead corpse.

Tarrell heard the speech as it came through half fainted ears, and she knew her loyalty to Devell was beyond repair, but she wanted to live. She wanted to live at least another day, hoping he'd somehow find it in his heart to forgive her. She laid there beside Big-O unable to move, with her eyes fixed on Devell as she tried to speak.

"Baby, I'm sorry, I never meant to...."

"BOC, BOC, BOC, BOC, BOC!" was the sound of the five shots that Devell sent through Tarrell's heart.

"There's no forgiveness for disloyalty!" he said as he turned to face his main man, falling to one knee, about to crumble in half from the pain he was still in. King George rushed to his side and helped his nigga up. "So what's up now fam?" asked King George, wondering what the fuck his main man was going to do about all the dead bodies in his muthafuckin' yard.

"You said you came to get me, right? Well, let's go. Take me to New York!"

Chapter 33

2 years later...

"Hey there gurl, what's up with you? I know you're going to the all-white ball tonight?!" asked Terrica, as she caught Do'Monique between classes in the hallway.

"I don't know bitch, you know I'm not big on that hanging out stuff, and besides, I have to study for my physics class. Mid Terms again." replied Do'Monique to her best friend...well, her best friend in New York.

Ever since she moved from Florida life has been different. She was attending college at the University of Buffalo. She looked totally different. She was still drop dead gorgeous, the past couple of years has allowed her to mature in every aspect of her appearance. Even the cosmetic surgery she had performed on her had reached its full potential. She loved the new look, it made her a total different person.

"Please, please, please Do'Monique, you have to go! How else am I going to get there?" begged Terrica, knowing Do'Monique uncle was going to let her push the

Benz, and being that Do'Monique still wasn't familiar with New York, she was guaranteed to be assigned designated driver. That's why she had to do whatever it took to get Do'Monique to go.

"I don't know! You know how them parties never be over with until the next afternoon!" added Do'Monique, really not wanting to go.

"I promise we'll leave early and I'll come back home with you so it won't be out of the way trying to take me home!"

They both stood still in the hallway as they looked at each other. Terrica was pleading her case as she waved her hands up and down begging, looking like she was trying to dry some freshly painted nails.

"Alright Bitch! But I promise you, I'm out before two-thirty."

"OOOOOHHH! Thank you, thank you, thank you so much! I'll be ready whenever you ready, just make sure to come and get me."

"Gurl, I'm not going to forget about you. It won't be a party without my muthafuckin' road dawg!" exclaimed Do'Monique.

"Oh shit, I gotta get to class!" warned Terrica as she looked at her watch and noticed she was five minutes late for African American studies class.

"Bitch, I'm late too!" said Do'Monique as she took off, but not before she heard her best friend's voice track her down.

"Don't forget to come and get me!"

Do'Monique just shook her head. Her friend was a

straight comedian, but she like her. Terrica reminded her of a Florida girl. Even though she had love for Terrica and trusted her, it was still some things that she just couldn't reveal to her friend, like the real reason she had come to New York. Her real name, and so forth. It was just about time she made her presence known in New York, and she was as ready as ever. Her hair had grown pass her shoulders and she was loving it.

"Hello Do'Monique!" she said to her new self, loving every moment.

****

There was an outstanding warrant in Florida for Devell, he was wanted for multiple counts of murder. He's even been featured on America's Most Wanted. Nobody knew of his whereabouts. Well, at least nobody beside King George and his plug.

Two years had done past and in that period of time, Devell had done made quite a name for himself. Well, not as Devell, but as 'Swift'. There wasn't no slowing down either. Once he regained his strength he began to mix in and out of the New York underworld, putting in work and gaining the streets trust. King George had other plans for his best friend. He wanted to introduce him to the elite class of bosses and players. He had a vision so vicious if only Devell would follow suit, they could take over New York. Devell's actions wasn't nothing new. He's been rebellious all their life, all he was able to do was have his main man's back. It didn't take long for Devell to take over the drug trade. New York niggas needed it and Florida niggas had it. His first shipment was for seventy-two birds. He didn't have the first bit of drugs to supply such a huge order, but he knew exactly where to get it from.

Once he convinced his New York niggas to front him the money, that was all it took for Devell to give Jamaican Maxwell a call. Maxwell couldn't believe it, nobody could find the young gangsta, and here he was talking on the phone with him. They set up a deal that would be repeated every two weeks. Devell had twenty-three niggas money in his possession, he was charging them all twenty-five grand a piece for each brick, rather than the going price of thirty thousand they were asking in New York. Maxwell was showing Devell some mad love, letting him get them thangs for seventeen grand flat. The only thing about it was Devell wasn't about to hit up Polk County ever again unless it was in a pine box. He set it up so one of his soldiers he had recruited could make the trip and do the deal.

That shit went like clockwork, it was like sunshine in the winter. Devell had done made millions of dollars beyond his imagination. The name Swift was like God to them. Every nigga he fucked with, if they wasn't on top, it didn't take long to get there once they plugged in with him. The biggest event of the year had come around. For any and everybody in New York, the place to be was Puff Daddy's all white party that was being held at his mansion up in the Hampton's. It was by special invite only, and being that King George had recently closed on a deal with Puffy, making him a silent partner in Puffy's new liquor brand, automatically gave him an all access pass to the whole extravaganza allowing him to invite a guest of his choice, which he chose his main man Devell.

The two childhood friends damn near looked like twins with the all-white tailored suits on both by different designers. Devell had a freshly shaved bald head, with his beard neatly trimmed. His teeth was as white as snow. That was his first priority once he got himself established in New York, to get his gold teeth removed and rebuild his grill with Ivory. On the other hand, King George was the complete opposite. He was never getting rid of his gold grill. If anything, he'd upgrade his shit, like he already done did twice, changing his yellow gold to platinum and diamonds, then back to rose gold with the diamonds and rubies. He was corporate thuggin' for real and his grill complimented his entire being. He had a fresh ass haircut, a number two, which was the lowest he ever went. It was the perfect length for him to display his full head of waves. He also had his beard neatly trimmed all nice and thin, looking like the debonair he was. It was show time for the two certified gangstas turned business men to get acquainted like never before. Finishing up his preparation, King George slung the white fur scarf around his neck as he yelled out to his main man.

"It's that time! I know you're ready!"

"Nigga, I been ready. It's your slow ass that's holding us up!" replied Devell.

"Whatever, I'll be waiting in the garage, since I'm the slow one."

Devell grabbed the box of Magnums and put them inside his suit jackets inner pocket. He knew he was about to get loose and get his freak on tonight and he wasn't trying to get caught slippin'. Heading out of the crib, Devell set the alarm as he entered the garage and jumped in the passenger seat of the new Bentley Bentayga, a birthday gift he had got for King George only a month ago. This was the first time they was taking the SUV out and they wanted it to be memorable. So why not shit on everybody at Puff Daddy's all white ball, where everybody and their momma was going to be at.

"You strapped?" asked King George, knowing they had to always be prepared. Nobody could be trusted when it came to your life.

"Hell yea I'm strapped. I got a whole box of Magnums in my coat!" said Devell being a smart ass while pulling out the gold and black box of condoms, waiving it in the air.

"Muthafucka, I ain't talking 'bout no damn rubbers. I'm talking about that heater! I know you ain't slippin' on me!"

"Nigga, I know what the fuck you was talking about! You know I don't go nowhere without my shit." said Devell, reaching into the small of his back revealing a plastic made .357 revolver which was the newest technology in the firearms department.

"Oh, okay! That's what's up fool! You know how these New York cats get when a nigga stunt on them."

"FUCK THESE NEW YORK NIGGAS! They better recognize a gangsta from pussy, because the first time a nigga try to get at me sideways, I'm burning up the whole spot."

King George knew first hand that his main man meant every word he uttered, and he was gon' back him up one hundred percent whether he's right or wrong. Pulling out of the five-car garage, he checked the rearview to make sure the garage door went down before they got caught up into the night. Seeing the S600 Benz Maybach, and the SL550 2 door disappear as the door made it to the ground. He had wanted to sell the two whips but Devell insisted on keeping them, it reminded him of the disloyalty his bitch Tarrell and his old homie Big-O portrayed before he saw them die.

The Bentley SUV looked flawless as it turned out of the driveway of the enormous twelve thousand square foot estate, making the twenty-eight inch rims and tires spew up water off the slightly wet road. They were forty-five minutes away from the Hampton's, those minutes was well worth it as the two friends found time to catch up on a lot of shit, especially since they were both headed in different directions.

****

Terrica had pulled up in Do'Monique's uncle silver Benz that was sitting pretty on some twenty-fours. She felt empowered behind the wheel of the big sedan, hopefully a nigga would think she was rolling like this and wanted to fuck with her. She was tired of fucking them broke ass college boys at her school. It was time a nigga held her down.

Do'Monique couldn't believe that she was actually at Puffy's all white party. When her friend Terrica first mentioned she had a way to get them in, she thought her friend was just on some bull shit. But when she showed back up with the two invites, she was looking forward to this day to come. She didn't have no damn test coming up, that was all a lie to keep control over the situation. She knew exactly what she was doing, and ain't no way in hell she was about to show her overall excitement. They were finally there. The valet greeted the two of them in a polite manner, giving them a parking ticket to retrieve their car when they got ready to leave.

Instantly all eyes were on Do'Monique. She had stolen the show instantly and the good thing about it was that nobody knew who the fuck she was, which was just how she liked it. The tight fitted white Moschino mini dress looked like it was trying to peel itself up off her. Her light skinned looked flawless as it glowed in the night's air as she strutted the red carpet into the premises of Puffy's Hampton's Estate.

TMZ, Vibe, Hip Hop Weekly, Don Diva, The Source, and Straight Stuntin photographers were present, snapping away, not missing a single thing. They had exclusive access to the whole event, and they had plans on taking complete advantage of the opportunity. These two divas they were witnessing had to be of some sort of celebrity status if only at least a video vixen. Terrica was in acting mode, she had plans on faking it until she made it. The all-white suit jacket and thigh level skirt gave her that professional look. She wasn't stacked like Do'Monique but she was damn sure holding her own. Her white and black heritage gave her a distinguished look that said "Wifey!" all day. And Terrica was hoping she could make somebody wife her for real after tonight.

They were being escorted to their V.I.P. tables.

Do'Monique wondered how in the hell her friend pulled all this off, but she wasn't about to ask. If she wanted her to know, she felt she would've told her. Do'Monique damn near lost her cool, their table was right next to Faith Evans table, and she was the biggest Faith Evans fan in the world. Not because of her music, because to her Faith had some really good music. It was where she came from that stood out to Do'Monique. She was from Polk County Florida. Even though they wasn't from the same city, both their cities sat inside of the same county and that's all that mattered to Do'Monique and if she was offered the opportunity tonight, she planned on letting it be known that her and Faith were home girls.

"Oh shit bitch, we got Champagne!" blurted out Terrica as she grabbed the chilled bottle and popped the top, pouring herself a glass then one for Do'Monique as well.

"Let's make a toast bitch!" she added.

"A toast to what?" asked Do'Monique, making Terrica pause in silence only for a second.

"Okay, I got it...let's toast to our come up!" she said raising her glass.

"To our come up!" agreed Do'Monique as she held her glass of Champagne up to Terrica's making the two crystal glasses kiss in the air.

The night was going more than planned. Nigga after nigga was trying their hand. Everybody wanted a piece of Do'Monique, and as bad as Terrica was, she still came up off just the friends. She had loved when Floyd Mayweather approached Do'Monique because his friend 50 Cent automatically went to talking to her. She knew exactly who Fifty was, and all he had to do was think it and she would do it, even if the request was beyond disgust.

Artist after artist took turns performing. Do'Monique was enjoying herself. This was the best time she ever had in her life. The Champagne had done kicked in and she wanted to dance. The music vibrations had her body heating up.

"Come on Terrica, come and dance with me?!"

"Hold up!" said Terrica as she grabbed the Champagne glass and downed another glass. "I'll suck a nigga dick right here, right now!" she thought to herself as she followed Do'Monique to the dance floor that was created in the huge yard. While they marched through the crowded yard, Do'Monique bumped into a group of niggas that looked like they were the most important muthafuckas at the party. If it wasn't for King George catching his main man Devell, he probably would've been knocked down.

"I'm so sorry, excuse me, I didn't mea..." and she was stuck, ain't no way she was seeing what she was seeing. He was standing right in front of her. She dreamed of him many of nights, and even though he tried to kill her, the feeling of his big ass dick banging her from the back stole all other thoughts of him. She wasn't about to take off and run for her life, because she didn't know if he would try to kill her again. But she was stuck, looking like a gorgeous deer stuck in a set of headlights.

"Are you okay?" asked King George as he admired the beautiful face in front of him. "Damn she looks familiar!" he thought as he awaited her response.

"Oh yea, I'm sorry...I just had a little too much to drink." Terrica not knowing the half, automatically jumped on Devell, making it a two on two, leaving her friend to deal with this blast from her past.

"This has to be him. He just looks like him!" she thought as she tried to keep her composure.

"Do you wanna sit down or something? Can I get you a juice or some Tylenol and water?" asked King George, putting his smooth, sensitive, I do care game down on her.

"No, I'm good. I was just about to go and dance before I accidently bumped into your friend."

"What, you're asking me to dance? Because if so, you're out of luck beautiful, I don't dance period."

Do'Monique was stuck on this nigga like glue. She was all in his grill, trying to read his dental. "This had to be him. Ain't no way in hell somebody looks this much alike. And he don't even recognize me. Oh my God, he can't tell who I am!" thought Do'Monique knowing she looked like a total different person after the surgery. She couldn't help but smile. Here this nigga was, the same nigga who tried to kill her in Florida, and didn't have a clue who she was. Do'Monique smile quickly turned from friendly to devious as she imagined getting her revenge, a revenge this nigga would never see coming.

"So, what's your name and where are you from?" asked Do'Monique.

"My name is King George and I'm from Florida!"

"Oh wow! Florida! I always wanted to visit Florida. I heard it was so beautiful there, and it's always sunny." she said being funny.

"Yea, it's beautiful and the sun is always shinning. Maybe I can take you there one day!" King George added, trying to blow her head up, knowing all New York broads wanted to go to Florida.

"For real, you'll take me to Florida?" expressed Do'Monique all excitedly, trying to make it seem like it was a lifelong dream of hers as well.

"Yea beautiful, if you act right!"

"And, what do you mean by that, if I act right?"

"Nothing serious, just saying if you was worth it, I'll take you to more places than just Florida!"

"Oh really?"

"I don't do no faking, try me and find out!" said King George cockily.

"Hold up, hold up, hold up...I done told you my name, now what's yours?" he asked, knowing she was going to give him a fake one at first. All hoes played that game but it was okay because he wasn't thinking about getting to know this bitch past tonight anyways, he only wanted to fuck her brains out and be on his way.

Do'Monique didn't know whether to tell this nigga her new name or her real name, what did she have to lose with either or.

"Oh, you too good to tell me your name?" asked King George, more impatiently. He noticed the deep dimples she had and it turned him on, he instantly got a hard on. "Damn this bitch look so familiar!" he thought as he took a sip of the orange juice he had nursing in his hand for the longest.

"You know what, if you want to act like that then be like that, I'll just call you Ms. Beautiful!" teased King

George.

"No, it's not that! I'm just funny about giving strangers my name!"

"Do I look like I'll bite?"

"I don't know, looks could be deceiving!" said Do'Monique, knowing first hand that this nigga in front of her was a stone-cold killer.

"Trust me, I'm the perfect gentleman! I won't bite and I won't let nobody hurt you."

"Well, since you put it that way, my name is Asia!"

TO BE CONTINUED...

Sneak Peak Of Treason 2

Damion had sucked the streets of Panama City, Florida dry. He didn't let a muthafucka get away with one penny. He took change, dollars, your food stamps benefit card and all. He was up there to get money and nothing else mattered. Damion had done went through six of the seven kilos' that he had got from the Tenille lick. He had broke each one down and grinded it out by the grams, making over one hundred thousand dollars off each brick. He figured in the next couple of days he'd be finish with his last one and off to Atlanta, Georgia he was going. He was finishing up breakfast with the tall black bitch Emma. She was his out of town pussy whenever he came to town. Right now, Emma had invited Damion to breakfast at Denny's and he was finished with his meal. He didn't have much time to waste on extra shit, it was time for him to get back to the money. Before he could get out of his seat comfortably, his phone goes off. Damion grabbed it out of his inside jacket pocket and read the caller I.D. screen. It was his cousin Trilla, "She must have a big sale nearby and needed him to make it!" He hurried and answered the phone.

"Hello?" But no one replied, "Hello?" Still no answer, "Cuz, why in the fuck is you playing on my phone?" barked Damion through the phone with anger in his voice. Still no answer, but he was able to hear someone talking in the background. He placed his hand over the mouth piece so he could hear what the hell was going on.

"She must've accidently called me and didn't even know it!" thought Damion as he sat back down in the Denny's booth eavesdropping on his cousin.

"Listen to me, and listen to me carefully! You have less than forty-eight hours to deliver us Damion. If not, then you're going away for a very long time!"

"I told you I got him. He thinks I got this square from Alabama who wants a brick of cocaine for forty thousand dollars. That's where you all come in at, you should be able to handle it from there, don't you think?" replied Trilla knowing that if she didn't deliver her cousin to the feds, it was her ass they were taking instead. She felt stupid after trying to flip her ex's drugs. Instead, she got popped and was released out on a snitch bond. Unfortunately, her cooperation with the feds landed her ex Dontae Spurlin twelve years in prison.

"I know this bitch ain't trying to set me up! I guess God does work in mysterious ways." he thought ironically at how her phone magically called him. "I guess I gotta bake a cake for my own fuck ass cousin and teach her 'bout fucking with a gangsta sideways!" Damion continued as he looked across the table booth at Emma, wondering if she had the slightest ideal about what Trilla was trying to do to him.

"Let's slide shawty, I'm ready to get back to the spot!" confessed Damion, knowing he didn't have time to do any fucking around with them peoples on his trail.

Once they made it back, him and Emma went inside and went about their business like everything was fine.

"Hey there cuz, did y'all bring me something back to eat?" asked Trilla, already knowing where they freaky asses were.

"You better ask your girl Emma. You know I don't be with all that shit!" expressed Damion in his normal tone, trying not to show his anger towards Trilla. He didn't want to tip her off to what he was about to do.

"You with that bullshit cuz......EMMMMA!!!" screamed out Trilla at her best friend. "Bitch, you better have brought me back something to eat!"

Emma didn't respond back, she was in the middle of pissing and needed to concentrate. She had to laugh to herself because she knew Trilla had to be hungry as hell after all the weed smoking they did last night before her and Damion crept away.

"Fuck both of y'all!" yelled out Trilla as she turned around about to head into the kitchen and cook her a breakfast sandwich but was stopped in her tracks as the barrel of Damion's .9mm pressed up against her forehead. She was stuck, unable to speak because she didn't know whether or not if Damion was playing or what.

"Bitch, you was gon' flip me! Your fuck ass fuckin' with those people with yo' police ass!" barked Damion in a menacing tone, one that let Trilla know she had been caught up in her shit. Trilla didn't know how in the hell Damion knew she was working with the feds trying to set him up. She didn't want to die. But knowing her cousin, with the look on his face, he was going to kill somebody.

"Please cuz, don't shoot me! Let me explain.... PLEASE!!" begged Trilla as tears began to pop out of both her eyes.

"You know me better than that cuz, I'll see you in hell bitch!" spoke Damion as he squeezed the trigger releasing a single round, "BOC!" into Trilla's head, killing her instantly.

Emma heard the gunshot as it echoed throughout the house, she didn't know what the fuck to think of it. She hoped like hell Damion ain't hurt himself or Trilla didn't do anything stupid because they didn't get her any food. Emma rushed out of the bathroom ready to give them both a tongue lashing, except she was stopped in her tracks once she saw Trilla spreaded out onto the floor in a pool of blood as it continued to ooze out of her head.

"NOOOOOOOOOOOOOO!!" she screamed before she was able to look up, but when she did it was like she went mute. Emma's pain and sorrow for her best friend turned into rage once her eyes laid on Damion. Emma knew that her fate could possibly be the same as Trilla's, but she didn't give a fuck. Here it was, her best friend was laying dead on the floor. The fucked up part about it all was, the muthafucka who killed her was her own cousin, someone she idolized. Emma took off in a charge towards Damion. In her mind, if she was just able to get her hands around his neck! But none of what she thought mattered because Damion was too swift as he leaned the .9mm in on her and squeezed the trigger letting off three rounds, "BOC! BOC! BOC!" Emma was dead before she knew it as her body made a free fall straight to the floor, right beside Trilla's.

Damion knew the neighbors had to have heard the gunshots and it was only a matter of time before the police showed up. He grabbed all of his money, the last kilo of cocaine, the lil clothes he had there and rushed to his car. He saw the lawn mower out front with the gas can sitting beside it. Damion quickly rushed to it and ran back inside and drenched both Trilla and Emma's body. He then lit a Newport, taking a pull on it before flicking it onto the gas drenched bodies. Once inside of his car Damion waited until he saw the flames blazing inside of the house through the window. He knew he was good as he crunk up the black Dodge Challenger and headed home. He was going back to Polk County, fuck going to Atlanta. He needed to be somewhere familiar and didn't give a fuck who liked it or not. Nobody was about to run him away from the streets that raised him.

ABOUT THE AUTHOR

Robert George III, born and raised in Winter Haven, Florida. He went from the Street Life to the High Life, experiencing the highs and the lows of the game. Robert tried with all of his might to leave the mean and deadly streets that raised him behind. Unfortunately, what he didn't know was that the streets wasn't ready to let go of him. He dodged every bullet sent his way as he fought to stay alive but didn't realize his demise from the outside world was lurking nearby.

Feeling the wrath of his right hand man's betrayal, Robert was set up by a Federal Informant which cost him his freedom, his beautiful life, his businesses, and all the material things that he had come to love so much. But God wasn't finished with Robert. As a matter of fact, he was just getting started. Having a passion for hustling, He discovered the book game was just like the dope game, but legal. Once he learned the in's and out's of it all, he jumped in head first. With thirteen books already written and four of them published, his goal is to be recognized as the greatest urban street story teller ever. Plus, he's the CEO of his own book publishing imprint "Trap House Publications 863". The same way he built an empire and ruled the streets, is the same way he's aiming to do with the publishing world.

Order Form

$14.95

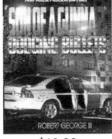
$13.99

$12.99

$14.99

$13.99

Name:_____

Address:_____

City:_____   State:_____
Zip:_____

Amount		Book Title or Pen Pal Number	Price
		Included for shipping for 1 book	**$4** U.S. / **$9** Inter

This book can also be purchased on:
AMAZON.COM/ BARNES&NOBLE.COM/ CREATESPACE.COM

We Help You Self-Publish Your Book

**You're The Publisher And We're Your Legs.
We Offer Editing For An Extra Fee, and Highly
Suggest It, If Waved, We Print What You Submit!**

Crystell Publications is not your publisher, but we will help you self-publish your own novel.

Don't have all your money? .... No Problem!
Ask About our Payment Plans
Crystal Perkins-Stell, MHR
Essence Magazine Bestseller
We Give You Books!
PO BOX 8044 / Edmond – OK 73083
www.crystalstell.com
(405) 414-3991
Don't have all your money up-front.... No Problem!

Ask About our Awesome Pay What You Can Plans

Plan 1-A 190 - 250 pgs $719.00	**Plan 1-B 150 -180 pgs $674.00**

Plan 1-C 70 - 145pgs $625.00

2 (Publisher/Printer) Proofs, Correspondence, 3 books, Manuscript Scan and Conversion, Typeset, Masters, Custom Cover, ISBN, Promo in Mink, 2 issues of Mink Magazine, Consultation, POD uploads. 1 Week of E-blast to a reading population of over 5000 readers, book clubs, and bookstores, The Authors Guide to Understanding The POD, and writing Tips, and a review snippet along with a professional query letter will be sent to our top 4 distributors in an attempt to have your book shelved in their bookstores or distributed to potential book vendors. After the query is sent, if interested in your book, distributors will contact you or your outside rep to discuss shipment of books, and fees.

Plan 2-A 190 - 250 pgs $645.00	**Plan 2-B 150 -180 pgs $600.00**

Plan 2-C 70 - 145pgs $550.00

1 Printer Proof, Correspondence, 3 books, Manuscript Scan and Conversion, Typeset, Masters, Custom Cover, ISBN, Promo in Mink, 1 issue of Mink Magazine, Consultation, POD upload.

We're Changing The Game.
No more paying Vanity Presses $8 to $10 per book!

Made in the USA
Coppell, TX
17 September 2021